Uncle's Dream

Uncle's Dream

Fyodor Dostoevsky

Translated by Hugh Aplin

Published by Hesperus Press Limited
19 Bulstrode Street, London W1U 2JN
www.hesperuspress.com

This translation first published by Hesperus Press Limited, 2011
Introduction and English language translation © Hugh Aplin, 2011

Designed and typeset by Fraser Muggeridge studio
Printed in Jordan by Jordan National Press

ISBN: 978-1-84391-208-8

CONTENTS

INTRODUCTION

The origins of what would eventually become *Uncle's Dream* seem to date back to 1855, when Fyodor Dostoevsky was living in the remote Siberian town of Semipalatinsk. Having completed the term of incarceration imposed for his involvement with the socialist Petrashevsky Circle, he was by then in the army, serving the customary period of exile imposed upon Russian political prisoners, be they Tsarist or Soviet, and longing to get back to the literary world from which he had been so cruelly wrenched at the end of the previous decade. 'I jokingly began a comedy,' he wrote to a friend, the poet Apollon Maikov, on 18 January 1856,

> and jokingly summoned up such a comic setting and so many comic figures, and was so pleased with my hero that I abandoned the form of a comedy, despite the fact that it was proving successful, specifically for the pleasure of following the adventures of my new hero and laughing out loud at him myself for as long as possible. The hero is somewhat akin to me. In short, I'm writing a comic novel, but up until now I'd just been writing separate adventures, I've written enough, and now I'm *sewing it all together* into a whole.

To what extent the author was referring here to *Uncle's Dream* and to what extent to *The Village of Stepanchikovo and its Inhabitants* is unclear. Both of these works, which followed one another into print in quick succession in 1859, are light-hearted in a way that readers of both his early writings and his later major novels might find surprising. But the idea that he was thinking more of the former is supported firstly by the fact that the word 'comedy' is used repeatedly in *Uncle's Dream* to refer to the events being described (the work has, indeed, been adapted for the stage more than twenty times over the years, bearing witness to its inherently dramatic structure); and secondly by Dostoevsky's fondness in the 1860s for adopting the persona of the eponymous uncle, the hero with whom he felt a perhaps surprising kinship: 'he could talk for hours on end,' wrote his second wife, Anna Grigoryevna, 'in the words and thoughts of his hero, the old prince from *Uncle's Dream*.'

The reason for a work of this nature being Dostoevsky's way back into literature was expressed by the writer himself some years later, in 1873, when he was asked to rework it for the stage: 'I wrote it then in Siberia, for the first time after hard labour, solely with the aim of starting my literary career again, and while terribly afraid of censorship (as a former exile). And thus I unwittingly wrote a little thing of dove-like mildness and remarkable innocence.' More than a decade on, Dostoevsky was harsh in his judgement of the piece, suggesting that it had enough in it for only a vaudeville, while there was 'insufficient content for a comedy, even in the figure of the Prince, the only serious figure in the entire tale'.

Dostoevsky was repeatedly critical of his own writings when reviewing them with hindsight, and the tenor of *Uncle's Dream* is so unlike that of the overwhelming majority of his oeuvre that his reservations about it were perhaps predictable – almost certainly more so than his characterisation of the Prince as a serious figure. How can this vain, forgetful, farcical character, whose behaviour is such that his relatives want him locked up, and who is at the very heart of the comic action of the story, be described by his creator as 'serious'? The answer presumably lies in his embodiment of a type within Russian society of the day that Dostoevsky included in his works with some regularity – the inadequate advocate of Western European cultural and political ideas, the ineffectual liberal with no true understanding of the Russia in which he sporadically lives. It was, of course, particularly appropriate for Dostoevsky to present readers with a ridiculous pastiche of a proponent of such 'new ideas' as the liberation of the serfs in a work at least in part intended to assure the authorities of his own political reliability. But if Prince K. is a ludicrous example of the 'Westerner' type, he can nonetheless be seen as an extreme, early variant of rather more significant portrayals, such as the figure of Stepan Verkhovensky in *The Devils* – a far greater work that yet has a number of things in common with *Uncle's Dream*.

Perhaps more surprising than his positive evaluation of the Prince is Dostoevsky's implicit dismissal of the other most striking figure in *Uncle's Dream*, the scheming mother, Maria Alexandrovna. Her lengthy dialogues with her daughter, Zina, and with Zina's would-be fiancé,

Mozglyakov, through which she contrives to bend each of these initially antipathetic interlocutors to her uncompromising will, are masterly expositions of persuasive power and cunning. Not for nothing is Maria Alexandrovna compared with Napoleon: not only does this comparison add substance to the mock-epic tone of the opening chapters, its effect is at the same time both comic (given the pettiness of her objectives and the limitations of her 'empire'), and also suggestive of Maria Alexandrovna's significance as an example of another type from Dostoevsky's world, namely, the strong, yet morally base character who fears no transgression in the pursuit of his or her aims. Of course, the name of Napoleon recurs most famously in the context of moral argument in the first of Dostoevsky's major novels, *Crime and Punishment*, and so again, a striking contribution to one of the writer's best-known and most significant ethical concerns can be seen to have been made in embryo in this ostensibly innocent minor comedy of provincial life.

Stylistically too, the reader finds in the pages of *Uncle's Dream* points of similarity with more renowned works. Employed here for the first time, for example, is a narrator who is very much a representative of the provincial setting he describes (and which Dostoevsky despised) – fond of gossip, eager for scandal, prone to hyperbole, partial, and seemingly at times not entirely in control of his material. A narrative point of view of this kind, together with the small-town backcloth of *Uncle's Dream* would be deployed again in each of Dostoevsky's final two novels, *The Devils* and *The Karamazov Brothers*. There too would be the brief time-span and consequent tight plot, as well as the exposition through dialogue, all of which perhaps stemmed from the genesis of *Uncle's Dream* as a comedy.

As well as looking forward, the work undoubtedly has echoes of aspects of Dostoevsky's pre-Siberian output too. In particular, in Vasya the impoverished teacher, the rival to Mozglyakov for Zina's affections, we are presented with another incarnation of the figure of 'the dreamer', so important in the author's tales of St Petersburg in the 1840s. How comfortably the fate and depiction of this literary relative of young Pokrovsky from *Poor People* fit into the overall scheme of *Uncle's Dream* is a matter for debate, but this is certainly a character with whose troubled type readers of Dostoevsky will be familiar – self-critical, self-analytical, and ultimately self-destructive.

Scholars have inevitably found numerous sources of inspiration for *Uncle's Dream*, most interestingly perhaps, considering the tale's origins, among works written for the Russian stage, either by such earlier writers as Denis Fonvizin, Alexander Griboyedov and Nikolai Gogol, or by Dostoevsky's contemporary Ivan Turgenev; some of Prince K.'s character traits and episodes from the plot surrounding him have even been linked with the tradition of Petrushka and the Russian puppet theatre, of which Dostoevsky was particularly fond. Yet this is a tale which, with the exception of the epilogue, depends for a full appreciation less upon the reader grasping literary allusions and references to contemporary Russia than do many of the great writer's other works. And what it therefore lacks in complexity, it makes up for in the directness of its appeal. The poet Alexei Plescheyev read the book before it was published, and in a letter to Dostoevsky of 10 February 1859, while expressing some reservations (especially about the depiction of the heroine, Zina), was unequivocal about its successes: 'The figure of Maria Alexandrovna is superb, magnificent. Mozglyakov… is an extremely accurate, lifelike figure. The provinces – in the persons of the ladies – are well-drawn too; some of the scenes with the Prince are so comical that one can't help laughing out loud.' This is not, then, Dostoevsky the archetypal gloomy Russian, but a Dostoevsky who belies that often mistaken reputation, and who might thus tempt readers to return to his other books with a new receptiveness to their not infrequent moments of comedy.

– *Hugh Aplin, 2011*

Uncle's Dream

(From the Chronicles of Mordasov)

CHAPTER I

Maria Alexandrovna Moskalyova is, of course, Mordasov's first lady, and of that there can be no doubt. She conducts herself as though she needs nobody, but rather, on the contrary, everybody needs her. True, hardly anybody likes her, and very many even sincerely hate her; but on the other hand everybody is afraid of her, and that is just what she wants. Such a requirement is in itself a sign of high politics. How, for example, is Maria Alexandrovna, who is terribly fond of gossip, and can't get to sleep all night if she hasn't learnt anything new the day before, how, for all that, is she able to conduct herself in such a way that it would never occur to you from looking at her that this majestic lady was the number one gossip in the world, or at least in Mordasov? On the contrary, you would think that gossip ought to vanish in her presence; gossips ought to blush and tremble like schoolchildren before their teacher, and conversation ought to proceed on none but the most lofty matters. She knows, for example, such capital and scandalous things about some Mordasovans that if at some suitable opportunity she were to tell them, and demonstrate them in the way she can demonstrate them, then there would be a Lisbon earthquake[1] in Mordasov. But in the meantime she is very taciturn about these secrets and would tell them only in the last resort, and then to none but her very closest lady-friends. She will only frighten one, hinting that she knows something, and likes keeping a man or a lady in constant fear better than striking the final blow. That's cleverness, that's tactics! Maria Alexandrovna has always been notable amongst us for her irreproachable *comme il faut*,[2] which everyone takes as their model. Regarding *comme il faut* she has no rival among the ladies of Mordasov. For example, she can murder, rip apart, annihilate a rival with a single word, something to which we can bear witness; yet at the same time she will pretend she hasn't even noticed uttering that word. And it's well known that such a characteristic is in itself an appurtenance of the very highest society. In general, in all such tricks she surpasses Pinetti himself.[3] Her connections are tremendous. Many of those visiting Mordasov have left in raptures over the reception she has given them and have later even conducted a correspondence with her. Someone even wrote some poetry for her, and Maria Alexandrovna showed it to everyone with pride. One visiting man of letters dedicated his novella to her, and he read it at a soiree she held as well, which produced an exceedingly pleasant effect. One German scientist, who came on purpose from Karlsruhe to study a particular kind of horned worm which is found in our province and who wrote four volumes *in quarto* about the worm, was so enchanted by Maria Alexandrovna's reception and courtesy that to this day he conducts a deferential and moral correspondence with her all the way from Karlsruhe. Maria Alexandrovna has even been compared, in a certain respect, with Napoleon. It goes without saying this was done in jest by her enemies, more for caricature than for the truth. But while fully acknowledging all the strangeness of such a comparison, I shall take the liberty, none-theless, of posing one innocent question: why, tell me, did Napoleon's head finally start to spin when he had climbed too high? Defenders of the old house ascribed it to the fact that not only was Napoleon not from the royal house, he was not even a *gentilhomme*[4] of good breeding; and for that reason, he naturally took fright in the end at his own height, and remembered his true place. Despite the obvious wit of this conjecture, reminiscent of the most brilliant times of the ancient French court, I shall take the liberty of adding in my turn: why will Maria Alexandrovna's head never on any account start to spin, and why will she always remain Mordasov's first lady? There have, for example, been instances when everyone has been saying: 'Well, and how will Maria Alexandrovna act now in such difficult circumstances?' But those difficult circumstances have come, and have gone, and – nothing! Everything has remained fine, as before, and even almost better than before. Everyone remembers, for example, how her spouse, Afanasy Matveyich, lost his job through his incapacity and feeble-mindedness, having incurred the wrath of a visiting government inspector. Everyone thought that Maria Alexandrovna would lose heart, demean herself, beg, implore – in short, let her wings droop. Nothing of the sort: Maria Alexandrovna realised that nothing more was to be gained by begging, and managed her affairs in such a way that she did not lose her influence on society in the least, and her house still continues to be considered the first house in Mordasov.

The public prosecutor's wife, Anna Nikolayevna Antipova, Maria Alexandrovna's sworn enemy (though outwardly her friend too), was already sounding victory. But when she saw how difficult it was to embarrass Maria Alexandrovna, she surmised that she had sunk her roots much deeper than had previously been thought.

Incidentally, since we've already mentioned him, we shall say a few words as well about Afanasy Matveyich, Maria Alexandrovna's spouse. Firstly, he is in appearance a most imposing man and even of very honest principles; but in critical instances he somehow becomes flustered and stares blankly like a sheep that has seen a new gate. He is extraordinarily majestic, especially at name-day dinners in his white tie. But all the majesty and imposingness is only until the moment when he starts to speak. And at that point, forgive me, you do well to plug your ears. He is positively unworthy of belonging to Maria Alexandrovna; that is the universal opinion. He held his job solely through the genius of his spouse. To my extreme mind, he should have gone into the kitchen garden to scare the sparrows long ago. There, and there alone, could he be of genuine, unquestionable use to his compatriots. And for that reason Maria Alexandrovna acted superbly in exiling Afanasy Matveyich to her village just outside of town, three versts[5] from Mordasov, where she has a hundred and twenty souls – to mention it in passing, the entire fortune, the entire means with which she so worthily maintains the nobility of her house. Everyone realised she had kept Afanasy Matveyich with her solely because he had been working and receiving a salary and… other income. And so when he stopped receiving the salary and the income, he was immediately sent away for his worthlessness and complete uselessness. And everyone praised Maria Alexandrovna for clarity of judgement and resolution of character. Afanasy Matveyich is in clover in the country. I dropped in on him and spent a whole hour with him quite pleasantly. He tries on white ties and personally cleans his own boots, not out of necessity, but solely out of a love of the art, because he likes his boots to shine; he drinks tea three times a day, is extremely fond of going to the bath-house, and – is content. Do you remember what a vile story blew up here about a year and a half ago regarding Zinaida Afanasyevna, Maria Alexandrovna and Afanasy Matveyich's only daughter? Zinaida is indisputably a beauty and superbly educated, but she is twenty-three and still not married. Amongst the reasons people give to explain why Zina is still not married, one of the main ones is considered to be those dark rumours about some strange relationship she had a year and a half ago with a wretched little teacher from a provincial town – rumours which have not ceased even now. To this day people talk about some kind of love letter written by Zina which was allegedly passed from hand to hand in Mordasov; but tell me: who has seen that letter? If it was passed from hand to hand, then where has it got to? Everyone has heard about it, but no one has seen it. I, at least, have met no one who has seen the letter with their own eyes. If you hint at all this to Maria Alexandrovna, she will simply refuse to understand you. Now suppose that there really was something, and Zina did write a note (I even think that it must have been so): what about the adroitness on Maria Alexandrovna's part! How well was an awkward, scandalous business suppressed, extinguished! Not a trace, not a hint! Now Maria Alexandrovna simply pays no attention to all that low slander; yet at the same time, she may have worked God knows how hard to keep the honour of her only daughter inviolate. And the fact that Zina is unmarried, well that's understandable: what suitors are there here? Zina could only possibly be married to a sovereign prince. Have you seen such a beauty of beauties anywhere? True, she is proud, too proud. They say that Mozglyakov is paying court, but there's unlikely to be a wedding. Who ever is Mozglyakov? True, he's young, not bad-looking, a dandy, has a hundred and fifty unmortgaged souls, is from St Petersburg. But I mean, firstly, he's not quite right in the head. A frivolous chatterbox with new ideas of some sort! And then what's a hundred and fifty souls, especially if you have new ideas! That wedding won't happen!

Everything that the gracious reader has now read was written by me about five months ago solely out of tender feelings. I confess in advance, I am somewhat biased towards Maria Alexandrovna. I wanted to write something of a eulogy to that magnificent lady and to present it all in the form of a playful letter to a friend, after the example of the letters once published in the old, golden, but, thank God, irretrievable days in *The Northern Bee*[6] and other periodical publications. But since I have no friend, and, what's more, have a certain innate literary timidity, my composition remained in my desk in the form of a literary trial of my pen, and as a memento of peaceful diversion in hours of leisure and amusement. Five months passed – and suddenly an amazing event occurred in Mordasov: early one morning Prince K. drove into town and put up at Maria Alexandrovna's house. The consequences of that visit were incalculable. The Prince spent only three days in Mordasov, but those three days left fateful and indelible memories. I'll say more: the Prince was the cause, in a certain sense, of a revolution in our town. The story of that revolution constitutes, of course, one of the most highly significant pages in the chronicles of Mordasov. And I finally resolved, after some hesitation, to polish that page in a literary manner and present it for the judgement of the highly respected public. My tale comprises the complete and remarkable story of the rise, the glory and the solemn fall of Maria Alexandrovna and all her house in Mordasov: a worthy and seductive theme for a writer. It stands to reason that first of all it is necessary to explain what is so amazing about Prince K. driving into town and putting up at Maria Alexandrovna's – and to do that, of course, it is also necessary to say a few words about Prince K. himself. I shall do just that. What's more, the biography of this figure is absolutely essential for the whole subsequent course of our story too. And so I set about it.

CHAPTER II

I shall begin with the fact that Prince K. was not yet God knows how old, but at the same time, when looking at him, you involuntarily got the idea that he might fall apart at any moment: so decrepit was he, or, to put it better, so worn out. Extraordinarily strange things of the most fantastic content were always told in Mordasov about this Prince. It was even said that the old man had gone crazy. Everyone thought it particularly strange that the owner of four thousand souls, a man with famous family connections, who might have had a significant influence in the province, had he wished, lived in isolation on his magnificent estate as an utter recluse. Many had known the Prince during his sojourn in Mordasov some six or seven years before and insisted that then he could not bear isolation and by no means resembled a recluse. However, here is everything reliable that I have been able to find out about him:

Once, in his young days, which was, though, very long ago, the Prince entered into life in a brilliant manner; he was a playboy, a philanderer, he ran out of money several times while abroad, sang romances, made puns and was never known for any brilliant intellectual capacity. It stands to reason that he plunged his entire fortune into disarray and, in old age, suddenly found himself almost without a kopek. Someone advised him to go to his village, which had already begun to be sold by public auction. He did, and arrived in Mordasov, where he lived for exactly six months. He found provincial life extraordinarily pleasing, and in those six months he squandered everything he had left, down to the last scrapings, continuing as a playboy and initiating various intimacies with provincial married ladies. He was, moreover, the kindest of men, although, it stands to reason, not without certain particular princely ways, which were considered in Mordasov, however, an appurtenance of the very highest society, and thus, instead of causing annoyance, even made an impression. The ladies in particular were in constant raptures over their nice guest. Many curious memories have survived. It was said, amongst other things, that the Prince would spend more than half the day at his toilette, and seemed to be entirely composed of various little bits. No one knew when or where he had managed to crumble so. He wore a wig, a moustache, side-whiskers and even an imperial – all false to the very last hair and a magnificent black colour; he used white powder and rouge daily. People insisted that he somehow smoothed out the wrinkles on his face with little springs, and that these springs were hidden in some special way in his hair. They also insisted that he wore a corset, because he had lost a rib when leaping clumsily out of a window somewhere during one of his amorous adventures in Italy. He limped on his left leg; people asserted that this leg was false, and that he had had the real one broken in some other adventure in Paris, but the new one he had had fixed on was some kind of special one made of cork. However, what won't people say? But it was true, nonetheless, that his right eye was a glass one, albeit very skilfully faked. His teeth too were made of composition. For days on end he would wash with various patented waters, would perfume and pomade himself. People remember, however, that the Prince was already beginning to grow noticeably decrepit then, and becoming unbearably garrulous. His career seemed to be coming to an end. Everyone knew that he no longer had a kopek. And suddenly, at that time, quite unexpectedly, one of his closest relatives, an extremely ancient old woman who had been permanently resident in Paris and from whom he could not possibly have expected an inheritance, died, having buried her legitimate heir exactly a month before her own death. Quite unexpectedly, the Prince had become her legitimate heir. The four thousand souls of the most magnificent estate exactly sixty versts from Mordasov passed to him alone, indivisibly. He immediately prepared to leave for St Petersburg to conclude his affairs. Seeing their guest off, our ladies gave him a magnificent subscription dinner. They remember that the Prince was charmingly jovial at this final dinner; he made puns, made people laugh, told the most extraordinary anecdotes, promised to come back to Dukhanovo (his newly acquired estate) as soon as possible, and gave his word that, upon his return, there would be uninterrupted festivities, picnics, balls, firework displays. For a whole year after his departure the ladies were talking about these promised festivities, awaiting their nice little old man with dreadful impatience. And while they were waiting, trips were even planned to Dukhanovo, where there was an old manor-house and garden, with lions clipped out of acacias, artificial tumuli, ponds across which floated boats with wooden Turks playing reed-pipes, summer-houses, pavilions, pleasure houses and other amusements.

Finally the Prince returned, yet, to universal surprise and disenchantment, he did not even call in at Mordasov, but settled at his Dukhanovo as a complete recluse. Strange rumours spread, and, in general, from this era on, the story of the Prince becomes obscure and fantastical. Firstly, it was said that he had not been entirely successful in St Petersburg, that some of his relatives, his future heirs, wanted, because of his feeble-mindedness, to get some kind of trusteeship over him, probably fearing that he would again squander everything. That wasn't all: some people added that they had even wanted to put him in the madhouse, but one of his relatives, an important gentleman, apparently stood up for him, demonstrating clearly to all the rest that the poor Prince, half-dead and half-false, would probably soon be completely dead, and then the estate would pass to them even without the madhouse. I repeat it once again: what won't people say, especially here in Mordasov? All this, so people said, was dreadfully alarming for the Prince, to the extent that he changed completely in character and turned into a recluse. Out of curiosity, some of the Mordasovans went to see him with their congratulations, but were either not received, or were received in an extraordinarily strange way. The Prince did not even recognise his former acquaintances. It was asserted that he didn't even want to recognise them. The Governor visited him too.

He returned with the news that, in his opinion, the Prince was indeed a little crazy, and afterwards he always pulled a sour face at the memory of his trip to Dukhanovo. The ladies were loudly indignant. One capital thing was finally found out, namely that the Prince was under the control of some unknown Stepanida Matveyevna, a woman of God knows what sort who had come with him from St Petersburg, elderly and fat, and who went around in cotton print dresses and with keys in her hands; that the Prince obeyed her in everything like a child, and didn't dare take a step without her permission; that she even washed him with her own hands; spoilt him, made a fuss of him and entertained him like a child; that, finally, it was she who kept all visitors away from him, and in particular the relatives, who had little by little been starting to drop in at Dukhanovo for reconnaissance purposes. There was much debate in Mordasov about this incomprehensible relationship, especially amongst the ladies. To all this was added the fact that Stepanida Matveyevna ran the Prince's entire estate in an unfettered and despotic manner; she dismissed stewards, bailiffs and servants, collected receipts; but she ran it well, so that the peasants blessed their lot. As far as the Prince himself was concerned, it was learnt that his days passed almost entirely with him at his toilette, trying on wigs and tailcoats; that he spent the rest of the time with Stepanida Matveyevna, playing my trumps with her, reading cards, and occasionally going out riding on a quiet English mare, when Stepanida Matveyevna would be certain to accompany him in a covered droshky, just in case – because the Prince rode mainly out of coquetry, and in reality could barely stay in the saddle. He was sometimes seen on foot as well, in an overcoat and a wide-brimmed straw hat with a lady's pink scarf around his neck, a glass in his eye and a straw basket on his left arm for collecting mushrooms, wild flowers, cornflowers; Stepanida Matveyevna always accompanied him on these occasions, while behind came two enormous footmen and, just in case, a carriage. And whenever a peasant encountered him and, stopping to one side, took off his hat, bowed low and kept on repeating: 'Hello, dear father Prince, Your Highness, light of our life!' the Prince would immediately direct his lorgnette at him, nod amicably and say to him affectionately: '*Bonjour, mon ami, bonjour*!'[7] And there were many similar rumours in Mordasov; it was quite impossible to forget the Prince: he lived in such close proximity!

So what was the universal astonishment when, one fine morning, the rumour spread that the Prince, the recluse, the eccentric, had come to Mordasov in his very own person and put up at Maria Alexandrovna's! Everything was thrown into commotion and agitation. Everyone awaited explanations, they all asked one another: what did it mean? Some were already preparing to drive to Maria Alexandrovna's. The Prince's arrival seemed a marvel to all. The ladies were sending notes to one another, preparing to call, despatching their chambermaids and husbands on reconnaissance missions. Precisely why the Prince had put up at Maria Alexandrovna's and not at anyone else's seemed especially strange. Most vexed of all was Anna Nikolayevna Antipova, because the Prince was in some way very distantly related to her. But in order to resolve all these questions, it's absolutely essential to drop in on Maria Alexandrovna herself, whom the gracious reader is welcome to visit too. True, it's still only ten o'clock in the morning now, but I'm sure she won't refuse to receive close acquaintances. At least, she's bound to receive us.

CHAPTER III

It's ten o'clock in the morning. We're in Maria Alexandrovna's house on Bolshaya Street, in the very room that, on grand occasions, the mistress calls her salon. Maria Alexandrovna has a boudoir too. The floor in this salon is reasonably well painted, and the specially ordered wallpaper isn't bad. In the furniture, which is quite clumsy, the predominant colour is red. There is a fireplace, above the fireplace a mirror, in front of the mirror a bronze clock with some kind of cupid in very bad taste. Between the windows, on the piers, are two mirrors, from which the time has been found to remove the covers. In front of the mirrors, on little tables, again there are clocks. By the rear wall is an excellent grand piano, ordered specially for Zina: Zina is a musician. Set out by the lighted fire, as far as possible in picturesque disorder, are some armchairs; in the midst of them is a small table. At the other end of the room is another table, covered with a tablecloth of dazzling whiteness; upon it are a boiling silver samovar and a pretty tea-service. In charge of the samovar and tea is a lady who lives with Maria Alexandrovna in the capacity of a distant relative, Nastasya Petrovna Zyablova.

Two words about this lady. She is a widow, she is past thirty, a brunette with a fresh complexion and lively dark-brown eyes. All in all, not bad-looking. She is of cheerful disposition and a great one for chuckling, she is quite sly, a gossip, of course, and she knows how to manage her affairs profitably. She has two children who are studying somewhere. She would very much like to marry again. She conducts herself quite independently. Her husband was an officer in the military. Maria Alexandrovna herself is sitting by the fire in the most excellent frame of mind and in a light-green dress, which suits her. She has been terribly gladdened by the arrival of the Prince who is at the moment sitting upstairs at his toilette. She is so glad that she doesn't even try to conceal her gladness. A young man standing in front of her is striking poses and recounting something in an animated way. It's clear from his eyes that he wants to please his listeners. He is twenty-five years old. His manners wouldn't be bad, but he often goes into raptures and, apart from that, has great pretensions to humour and sharp wit. He is very well-dressed, fair-haired, not bad-looking. But we've already spoken of him: this is Mr Mozglyakov, who promises much. Privately, Maria Alexandrovna finds him rather empty-headed, but she gives him an excellent reception. He is a suitor for the hand of her daughter Zina, with whom, according to him, he is madly in love. He continually turns to Zina, trying to pluck a smile from her lips with his wit and gaiety. But she is visibly cold and offhanded with him. At this moment she is standing to one side, by the piano, fingering a calendar. She is one of those women who excite universal rapturous amazement when they appear in society. She is impossibly pretty: a tall brunette with wonderful, almost completely black eyes, shapely, with a mighty, marvellous bust. Her shoulders and arms are classical, her little feet seductive, her gait regal. Today she is a little pale; but on the other hand, her plump little scarlet lips with their astonishing outline, between which, like a string of pearls, gleam her even, white teeth, will appear in your dreams for the next three days if you give them just one glance. Her expression is serious and severe. Monsieur Mozglyakov appears to be afraid of her steady gaze; at least, he sort of flinches whenever he dares to glance at her. Her movements are haughtily offhanded. She is wearing a simple, white, muslin dress. White suits her extraordinarily well; but then everything suits her. On her finger is a ring, woven out of someone's hair, and to judge by the colour, not her Mamma's; Mozglyakov has never dared ask her whose hair it is. This morning Zina is somehow especially taciturn, and even sad, as if preoccupied with something. Maria Alexandrovna, on the other hand, is prepared to talk incessantly, though she too occasionally throws a particular sort of suspicious glance at her daughter; she does so stealthily, however, as if she is afraid of her as well.

'I'm so glad, so glad, Pavel Alexandrovich,' she twitters, 'that I'm prepared to shout about it from the window to anyone and everyone. Not to mention the nice surprise you gave us, Zina and me, arriving two weeks earlier than promised; that goes without saying! I'm terribly glad that you've brought the dear Prince here with you. Do you know how I love that enchanting little old man? But no, no! You won't understand me! You young people won't understand my delight, no matter how much I assure you of it! Do you know what he meant to me in former times, some six years ago, do you remember, Zina? I forgot, though: you were staying with your aunt then... You won't believe it, Pavel Alexandrovich: I was his guide, his sister, his mother! He obeyed me like a child! There was something naive, tender and ennobled about our relationship; something even sort of pastoral... I really don't know what to call it. That's why he now remembers my house alone with gratitude, *ce pauvre prince*![8] Do you know, Pavel Alexandrovich, you may have saved him by bringing him to me! I've thought of him these six years with grief in my heart. You won't believe it: I've even dreamt about him. They say that monstrous woman has bewitched him, destroyed him. But at long last you've torn him from those clutches! No, we must make the most of the opportunity and save him completely! But tell me again, how did you manage it all? Describe your entire meeting to me in the most detailed manner. In my haste before, I only paid attention to the main thing, whereas all those little things, it's the little things that comprise, so to speak, the real juice! I'm terribly fond of the little things, even in the most important instances I pay attention to the little things first... and... while he's still sitting at his toilette...'

'Everything was just as I said before, Maria Alexandrovna!' Mozglyakov chimes in readily, prepared to tell the story even a tenth time – it's a delight for him. 'I travelled all night, and of course, was awake all night – you can imagine the hurry I was in!' he adds, turning to Zina, 'in short, I cursed, shouted, demanded horses, even kicked up a fuss over the horses at the posting stations; if it were published, it would make an entire narrative poem in the latest taste! Still, leaving that aside! At exactly six o'clock in the morning I arrive at the last station, at Ivashevo. Frozen through, I don't even want to warm myself, I shout: horses! Frightened the station-master's wife with a babe in arms: her milk's dried up now, apparently... An enchanting sunrise. You know, that frosty dust's scarlet and silver![9] I pay no attention to anything; in short, I'm in the devil of a hurry! I battled to get the horses: took them away from some Collegiate Councillor and all but challenged him to a duel. I'm told that a quarter of an hour before, some prince or other has left the station with his own horses, he'd spent the night. I'm scarcely listening, I get in and fly, as though I've broken free from a chain. There's something similar in Fet,[10] in some elegy or other.

'Exactly nine versts from town, right at the turning for the Svetozerskaya Hermitage, I see an amazing incident has occurred. An enormous travelling carriage is lying on its side, the coachman and two footmen are standing in front of it in bewilderment, while coming from this carriage that's lying on its side are heart-rending cries and shrieks. I thought of driving on by: you lie on your side; I'm not of this parish! But I was overcome by philanthropy, which, as Heine puts it, pokes its nose in everywhere.[11] I stop. I, my Semyon, the driver – a Russian soul too – we hurry to lend a hand and thus, the six of us, we finally raise the conveyance and set it on its feet, which, to tell the truth, it doesn't have, because it's on runners. Some peasants who were coming into town with firewood helped too, and I gave them something for vodka. I think: it's probably that same prince! I look: good heavens! It is indeed him, Prince Gavrila! What a way to meet! I shout to him: "Prince! Uncle!" Of course, he almost didn't recognise me at first glance; but then straight away he almost did… at second glance. I must admit to you, however, he barely understands even now who I am, and seems to take me for someone else, and not for a relative. I saw him about seven years ago in St Petersburg; well, of course, I was a little boy then. Yet I remembered him: I was struck by him – well, but how was he to remember me! I introduce myself; he's delighted, embraces me, but at the same time he's trembling all over with the fright, and crying, honest to God, crying: I saw it with my own eyes!

'After one thing and another, I finally persuaded him to get into my closed sleigh and drive to Mordasov, if only for a day, to cheer himself up and have a rest. He consents unquestioningly… Declares to me that he's going to the Svetozerskaya Hermitage to see Father Misail, whom he honours and respects; that Stepanida Matveyevna (and which of us relatives hasn't heard of Stepanida Matveyevna? – she drove me out of Dukhanovo with a mop last year), that this Stepanida Matveyevna had received a letter containing word that someone of hers in Moscow was at their last gasp: her father or daughter, I don't know who precisely, and I'm not interested in knowing either; perhaps both father and daughter together; perhaps supplemented by some nephew too, who's got a job connected with drink... In short, to such a degree was she in turmoil that she resolved to bid her Prince farewell for ten days or so and flew off to the capital to adorn it with her presence.

'The Prince sat for one day, then another, tried on his wigs, pomaded himself, dyed his facial hair, tried to read his cards (or maybe even his beans); but it became unbearable without Stepanida Matveyevna! He ordered his horses and drove off for the Svetozerskaya Hermitage. One of his people, fearing the invisible Stepanida Matveyevna, almost dared to raise an objection; but the Prince insisted. He drove off after lunch yesterday, spent the night at Ivashevo, left the station at dawn, and right at the turning for Father Misail almost flew into a gully with the carriage. I save him, persuade him to drop in on our mutual friend, the highly respected Maria Alexandrovna; of you he says that of all the ladies he has ever known, you are the most enchanting, and so here we are, and the Prince is now upstairs, setting his toilette to rights with the help of his valet, whom he didn't forget to take with him, and whom he never will under any circumstances forget to take with him, because he will sooner agree to die than present himself to ladies without certain preparation or, to put it better, adjustments... And that's the whole story! *Eine allerliebste Geschichte!*'[12]

'But what a humorist he is, Zina!' cries Maria Alexandrovna, after hearing him out, 'how nicely he recounts it! But Paul, listen – one question: explain to me properly how you're related to the Prince! You call him Uncle?'

'Honest to God, I don't know, Maria Alexandrovna, how and in what way I'm related to him: I'm a cousin seven times removed, apparently, or maybe not even a cousin, but something else. I'm not a bit to blame for it; it's Auntie Aglaya Mikhailovna who's to blame for it all. Still, Auntie Aglaya Mikhailovna has got nothing else to do besides counting up her relatives on her fingers; it was she who chucked me out to go and see him in Dukhanovo last summer. She should have gone herself! Quite simply, I call him Uncle; he responds. And that's all there is to our being related, at least for the present...'

'But I'll say it again anyway that God alone could have given you the idea of bringing him straight to me! I tremble when I imagine what would have become of him, the poor thing, if he'd ended up with someone else and not with me! He'd have been snapped up, torn to pieces, devoured! People would have leapt upon him as if upon a mine, as if upon a valuable mineral deposit – maybe they'd have robbed him? You can't imagine what greedy, low and sly little people there are here, Pavel Alexandrovich!…'

'Ah, good heavens, but to whom was he to be brought if not to you – what a one you are, Maria Alexandrovna!' chimes in Nastasya Petrovna, the widow pouring the tea. 'He's not going to be taken to Anna Nikolayevna, is he, what do you think?'

'Why is he taking so long to emerge, though? It's even strange,' says Maria Alexandrovna, rising from her seat in impatience.

'Uncle, you mean? Yes, I think he'll be there another five hours getting dressed! What's more, since he has absolutely no memory, he may even have forgotten that he's come to stay with you. He's the most astonishing person, you know, Maria Alexandrovna!'

'Oh, come, come, please, it can't be so!'

'Not "it can't be so" at all, Maria Alexandrovna, it's the absolute truth! I mean, he's half composition, not a person. You saw him six years ago, but I saw him an hour ago. I mean, he's half-dead! He's only a memory of a person, he is; they forgot to bury him! He has false eyes, you know, cork legs, he's all on springs, and he talks using springs too!'

'Good heavens, how frivolous you are, though, by the sound of you!' exclaims Maria Alexandrovna, adopting a stern air. 'And you should be ashamed, a young man, a relative, talking about that venerable old man in that way! Not to mention his unexampled kindness,' and her voice takes on a touching sort of expression, 'remember that he's a remnant, so to speak, a fragment of our aristocracy. My friend, *mon ami*, I understand that you're being frivolous because of these new ideas of yours of which you talk incessantly. But good heavens! I myself share your new ideas! I understand that your tendency is basically noble and honest. I sense that there's even something lofty in these new ideas; but all this doesn't prevent me from seeing the plain, so to speak, practical side of the matter too. I have lived in the world, I have seen more than you, and, finally, I am a mother, while you are still young! He is an old man, and for that reason, in your eyes, ridiculous! And that's not all: last time, you were even saying you intended setting your peasants free, and that you simply had to do something for the age, and it's all because you've read such a lot of this Shakespeare of yours! Believe me, Pavel Alexandrovich, your Shakespeare had his day ages ago, and if he were to rise from the dead, even with all his intelligence, he still wouldn't be able to make out a single line in our life! If there is anything chivalrous and majestic in our contemporary society, it's to be found precisely in the highest estate. A prince is a prince even in a paper bag, and even in a hovel a prince will be as in a palace! Whereas Natalya Dmitriyevna's husband has built himself practically a palace – yet he's only Natalya Dmitriyevna's husband all the same and nothing more! And Natalya Dmitriyevna herself, even if she sticks on fifty crinolines, will all the same remain the old Natalya Dmitriyevna and won't add anything to herself at all. You too are, in part, a representative of the highest estate, because you're descended from it. I too consider myself no stranger to it – and it's a bad child that soils its own nest! But anyway, you'll arrive at all this for yourself better than me, *mon cher Paul*,[13] and you'll forget your Shakespeare. I forecast it for you. I'm certain that even now you're not sincere, but are just being like it to follow fashion. However, I've let my tongue run away with me. Stay here, *mon cher Paul*, I'll go upstairs myself and find out about the Prince. Perhaps he needs something, and with my wretched servants...'

And having remembered about her wretched servants, Maria Alexandrovna left the room in a hurry.

'Maria Alexandrovna seems to be very glad that that flashy Anna Nikolayevna didn't get hold of the Prince. And she kept on claiming she was related to him, didn't she? She must be bursting with annoyance right now!' remarked Nastasya Petrovna; but remarking that there was no reply, and glancing at Zina and at Pavel Alexandrovich, Mrs Zyablova had the sense to leave the room at once, as if for a reason. She compensated herself immediately, however, by stopping outside the door and starting to eavesdrop.

Pavel Alexandrovich turned to Zina at once. He was dreadfully agitated; his voice was trembling.

'Zinaida Afanasyevna, are you angry with me?' he pronounced with an air of timidity and entreaty.

'With you? But what about?' said Zina, blushing slightly and raising her wonderful eyes to him.

'About my early arrival, Zinaida Afanasyevna! I ran out of patience, I couldn't wait another two weeks… I've even been dreaming about you. I've flown here to learn my fate… But you're frowning, you're angry! Am I even now not to learn anything definite?'

Zinaida was, indeed, frowning.

'I was waiting for you to start talking about this,' she replied, lowering her eyes once more; her voice was firm and stern, but in it could be heard annoyance. 'And since the wait was a very difficult one for me, the sooner it was concluded, the better. Again you're demanding, that's to say, asking for a reply. Very well, I'll repeat it to you, because my reply is still the same as it was before: wait! I repeat to you – I haven't made up my mind yet, and I can't promise you that I'll be your wife. It's not a thing that's demanded using force, Pavel Alexandrovich. But, to reassure you, I can add that I'm still not definitively refusing you. Note this too: giving you hope now of a favourable decision is something I do solely because I'm indulgent to your impatience and anxiety. I repeat that I wish to remain completely free in my decision, and if in the end I tell you that I don't consent, you shouldn't blame me for having given you hope. And so now you know.'

'And so what on earth, what on earth is this!' exclaimed Mozglyakov in a plaintive voice. 'Is this really hope? Can I derive any hope at all from your words, Zinaida Afanasyevna?'

'Remember all I've said to you and derive from it anything you like. It's up to you! But I shall add nothing more. I'm not yet refusing you, only saying: wait. But, I repeat to you, I'm reserving myself every right to refuse you, if I take it into my head to do so. I'll remark on one more thing, Pavel Alexandrovich: if you've come back for an answer earlier than the agreed time so as to operate in roundabout ways, hoping for third-party patronage, even, for example, for Mamma's influence, then you're much mistaken in your reckoning. In that case I'll refuse you point-blank, do you hear? But that's enough for now, and please, until the time comes, don't say a word to me about it.'

This entire speech was pronounced dryly, firmly, and without hesitation, as though it had been pre-learnt. Monsieur Paul felt he had been left high and dry. At that moment Maria Alexandrovna returned. And after her, almost immediately, Mrs Zyablova.

'It seems he'll be coming down straight away, Zina! Nastasya Petrovna, brew some fresh tea quickly!' Maria Alexandrovna was even a little agitated.

'Anna Nikolayevna has already sent to make enquiries. Her Anyutka came running to the kitchen and was asking questions. She must be cross now!' proclaimed Nastasya Petrovna, rushing to the samovar.

'What do I care?' said Maria Alexandrovna, answering Mrs Zyablova over her shoulder. 'As if I'm interested in knowing what your Anna Nikolayevna thinks! Believe me, I won't be sending anyone in secret to *her* kitchen. And I'm at a loss, simply at a loss as to why you all consider me that poor Anna Nikolayevna's enemy, it's not just you, but everyone in town. I'll refer the matter to you, Pavel Alexandrovich! You know both of us – so why should I be her enemy? Over being first? But I'm indifferent to this business of being first. Let her, let her be first! I'm the first to be ready to go to her and congratulate her on being first. And in the end – it's all unfair. I shall stand up for her, it's my duty to stand up for her! She is slandered. Why do you all attack her? She's young and loves fine clothes – is that why? But better fine clothes, in my view, than something else, as with Natalya Dmitriyevna, who loves such a thing that it can't even be mentioned. Is it because Anna Nikolayevna goes out visiting and can't stay at home? But good heavens! She hasn't had any education, and of course, it's hard for her to open a book, for example, or to keep herself busy with anything for two minutes at a time. She flirts and makes eyes through the window at everyone who goes down the street. But why do people assure her she's pretty, when all she has is a white face and nothing more? She makes you laugh when she's dancing, you must agree! But then why do people assure her she dances the polka splendidly? She wears impossible head-dresses and hats – yet how is she to blame if God gave her no taste, but, on the contrary, so much credulity? Assure her it's a good thing to pin a sweet wrapping to your hair and she'll pin one on. She's a gossip – but that's customary here: who here doesn't gossip? Sushilov with his side-whiskers visits her both morning and evening, and practically in the night-time too. Ah, good heavens, but of course: her husband used to be out playing cards until five o'clock in the morning! And besides, there are so many bad examples here! In the end it *may* still be slander. In a word, I shall always, always stand up for her!…

'But good heavens! Here's the Prince! It's him, him! I recognise him! I'd recognise him out of a thousand! I see you at long last, *mon prince*!' exclaimed Maria Alexandrovna, and rushed towards the Prince as he came in.

CHAPTER IV

At a first, cursory, glance, you wouldn't take the Prince for an old man at all, and only after looking closer and more intently would you see that he was a sort of dead man on springs. Every artistic means is used to dress this mummy up as a youth. An amazing wig, side-whiskers, moustache and imperial of the most excellent black colour cover half his face. The face is powdered white and rouged with extraordinary skill, and there are almost no wrinkles on it. Where they have got to is unknown. He is dressed in absolute accordance with fashion, as if he has broken out of a fashion illustration. He is wearing a sort of morning coat or something similar, honest to God, I don't know what exactly, only something extremely fashionable and modern, created for morning calls. The gloves, tie, waistcoat, linen and everything else – all is dazzlingly fresh and in elegant taste. The Prince limps a little, but limps so neatly, it's as though this too is an essential, to be in fashion. There is a glass in his eye, the very eye which is anyway made of glass. The Prince is drenched in perfume. When conversing, he kind of drawls out some of the words in particular – perhaps because of senile feebleness, perhaps because all his teeth are false, and perhaps for greater show. He pronounces some syllables with extraordinary sweetness, putting particular emphasis on the letter *e*. He makes *yes* come out sort of *yye-es*, only a little sweeter still. In his manner as a whole there is something offhanded, something studied over the course of all his life as a dandy. But generally, if there was anything preserved from that former life of his as a dandy, then by now it was preserved in a sort of unconscious way, like some vague memory, like some long gone, dead and buried olden days which, alas, no cosmetics, corsets, perfumers or hairdressers were going to revive. And for that reason we shall do best if we admit in advance that, if he has not yet lost possession of his faculties, the old man did lose his memory long ago and is continually getting confused, repeating himself, and even completely making things up. It even takes skill to talk to him. But Maria Alexandrovna has trust in herself and, at the sight of the Prince, goes into indescribable raptures.

'But you haven't changed at all, not at all!' she exclaims, seizing both her guest's hands and sitting him down in a comfortable armchair.

'Do sit down, do sit down, Prince! Six years, six whole years we haven't seen one another, and not a single letter, not even one single line in all that time! Oh, how at fault you are before me, Prince! How angry I was with you, *mon cher prince*! But – some tea, some tea! Ah, good heavens! Nastasya Petrovna, some tea!'

'My gratitude, gra-ti-tude, so at fa-ault! So-o at fa-ault!' lisps the Prince (we forgot to say that he lisps a little, but he does this too as though following fashion). 'And imagine, just last year I meant to come back here without fail,' he adds, examining the room through his lorgnette. 'But I was frightened off: there was cho-le-ra here, they say.'

'No, Prince, we didn't have cholera,' says Maria Alexandrovna.

'There was cattle plague here, Uncle,' Mozglyakov interjects, wishing to distinguish himself. Maria Alexandrovna measures him with a stern gaze.

'Why yes, ca-ttle plague, or something of the sort… And so I stayed where I was. Well, how is your husband, my dear Anna Nikolayevna? Still at his prosecu-tor's work?'

'N-no, Prince,' says Maria Alexandrovna, stammering a little. 'My husband isn't a pro-se-cutor…'

'I wager Uncle's got mixed up and takes you for Anna Nikolayevna Antipova!' cries quick-witted Mozglyakov, but he checks himself at once, noticing that even without these explanations Maria Alexandrovna seems to have been quite crushed.

'Why yes, yes, Anna Nikolayevna, oh no… (I forget everything!). Oh yes, Antipovna, precisely, Anti-povna,' the Prince confirms.

'N-no, Prince, you're very much mistaken,' says Maria Alexandrovna with a bitter smile. 'I'm not Anna Nikolayevna at all, and, I confess, I certainly didn't expect you not to know me! You've amazed me, Prince! I'm your friend from the past, Maria Alexandrovna Moskalyova. Do you remember Maria Alexandrovna, Prince?…'

'Maria A-lex-and-rovna! Imagine, I did indeed sup-pose you to be (what's her name?) – oh yes! Anna Vasilyevna… *C'est délicieux*![14] So I've come to the wrong place. And I thought, my friend, you were indeed ta-king me to that Anna Matveyevna. *C'est charmant*![15] However, it's often the case with me… I often go to the wrong place.

Overall I'm happy, I'm always happy, whatever happens. So you're not Nastasya Va-silyevna? That's in-teresting…'

'Maria Alexandrovna, Prince, Maria Alexandrovna! Oh, you should be ashamed of yourself! Forgetting your best, best friend!'

'Why yes, my best friend… *pardon, pardon!*' lisps the Prince, staring raptly at Zina.

'And this is my daughter, Zina. You haven't met before, Prince. She wasn't here at the time when you were, remember, in 18**?'

'This is your daughter! *Charmante, charmante!*' the Prince mumbles, examining Zina greedily through his lorgnette. '*Mais quelle beauté!*'[16] he whispers, clearly smitten.

'Some tea, Prince,' says Maria Alexandrovna, drawing the Prince's attention to the page who is standing in front of him with a tray in his hands. The Prince takes his cup and becomes lost in contemplation of the boy, whose little cheeks are plump and pink.

'A-a-ah, is this your boy?' he says. 'What a pre-tty boy!… A-a-and no doubt beha-ves… himself well?'

'But Prince,' Maria Alexandrovna hurriedly interrupts, 'I've heard about that most awful thing that happened! I confess I was beside myself with fright… You weren't hurt? Take care, you mustn't disregard it…'

'Overturned it, overturned it, the coachman overturned it,' the Prince exclaims with unusual animation. 'I was already thinking the end of the world was nigh or something of the sort, and I took fright so, I confess, that – saints forgive me – I thought the sky was going to come crashing down! I didn't expect it, didn't ex-pect it, didn't ex-pe-ct it at all! And it's my coachman Fe-o-fil who's to blame for it all! I'm relying on you in everything now, my friend: take charge and investigate it properly. I am cer-tain he was making an a-ttempt on my life.'

'Very well, very well, Uncle!' Pavel Alexandrovich replies. 'I'll investigate everything! Only listen, Uncle! You forgive him for today, eh? What do you think?'

'Not for anything will I forgive him! I am certain he was making an attempt on my life! He, and Lavrenty too, whom I left at home. Imagine: he's picked up some, you know, new ideas! He's got a sort of negative attitude about him… In a word: a communist, in the full sense of the word! I'm afraid even of meeting him!'

'Ah, what you've said is so true, Prince,' exclaims Maria Alexandrovna. 'You wouldn't believe how these good-for-nothing servants make me myself suffer! Imagine: I've just changed two of my servants and, I confess, they are so stupid that I'm simply battling with them from morning till evening. You wouldn't believe how stupid they are, Prince!'

'Why yes, why yes! But I confess, I even like a manservant to be stupid in part,' remarks the Prince, who, like all old men, is pleased when people show servility by listening to his chatter. 'It suits a manservant somehow – and even constitutes his me-rit if he is sincere and stupid. Only in some ca-ses, it stands to reason. There's somehow something more impo-sing about him as a result, there's a sort of sole-mnity in his face; in a word, something more well-mannered, and I demand of *a man* good ma-nners above all. Now I've got this Te-ren-ty. You remember Te-ren-ty, my friend, don't you? As soon as I looked at him, I predicted it from the very first: you're going to be a doorman! Phe-no-menally stupid! Stares at you like a sheep! But how impo-sing, what sole-mnity! His Adam's apple is light-pink, you know! Well, and in a white tie and all decked out it constitutes an effect, you know. I've come to love him dearly. There are times I look at him and can't tear my eyes away: he composes a positive dissertation – such a grand air! – in a word, the genuine German philosopher Kant,[17] or, to be even more exact, a plump, fattened turkey. Perfect *comme il faut*[18] for a serving man!…'

Maria Alexandrovna chuckles with the most rapturous enthusiasm and even claps her hands. Pavel Alexandrovich echoes her whole-heartedly: he finds his Uncle extremely interesting. Nastasya Petrovna began chuckling too. Even Zina smiled.

'But there's so much humour, so much gaiety, so much wit about you, Prince!' exclaims Maria Alexandrovna. 'What a precious ability to note the most subtle, the most amusing feature!… And disappearing from society, locking yourself away for five whole years! With such talent! But you could write, Prince! You could be a second Fonvizin, Griboyedov, Gogol!…'[19]

'Why yes, why yes!' says the completely contented Prince, 'I can be a se-cond… and you know, I was extraordinarily witty in the old days.

I even wrote a vau-de-ville for the stage... There were a number of de-light-ful stanzas in it! It was never acted, though...'

'Ah, how lovely it would be to read it! And you know, Zina, it would be just the time now! They're going to set up a theatre group in town, you know – for patriotic donations, Prince, in aid of the wounded...[20] your vaudeville would be just the thing!'

'Of course! I'm even prepared to write it out again... though I've completely forgo-tten it. But I remember there were two or three such plays on words that...' and the Prince kissed his hand. 'And in general, when I was abro-ad, I caused a ge-nuine *fu-ro-re*. I remember Lord Byron. We were on a friendly foo-ting. He danced the cracovienne delightfully at the Congress of Vienna.'[21]

'Lord Byron, Uncle! Pardon me, Uncle, but what are you saying?'

'Why yes, Lord Byron. Though maybe it actually wasn't Lord Byron, but someone else. Not Lord Byron at all, but a Pole! I can recall it fully now. And that Pole was high-ly or-i-gi-nal: passed himself off as a Count, but later on it transpired that he was some sort of chef. Only he danced the cracovienne de-light-fully, and in the end broke his leg. I composed some verse straight away at the time to mark the occasion:

Our Polish friend
Danced the cracovienne...

And then... and then what came next I can't remember...'

When his leg he did break
He did dancing forsake.

Well, mustn't that have been it, Uncle?' exclaims Mozglyakov, becoming more and more inspired.

'I think it must, my friend,' his uncle replies, 'or something si-milar. Though maybe not, only the verse was highly successful... Generally, I have forgotten certain occurrences now. It's because I'm so busy.'

'But do tell us, Prince, what have you been busy doing all this time in your solitude?' Maria Alexandrovna enquires. 'I've thought about you so often, *mon cher prince*, that, I confess, I'm burning with impatience on this occasion to learn about it in more detail...'

'What have I been doing? Well, generally, you know, I've been busy with lots of things. There are times you're resting; and sometimes, you know, I walk about, imagine various things...'

'You must have an extremely powerful imagination, Uncle?'

'Extremely powerful, my dear. I sometimes imagine such things that I'm even sur-pri-sed at myself later on. When I was in Kaduyev... *A propos*! You were Vice-Governor of Kaduyev, I think, weren't you?'

'Me, Uncle? Pardon me, what are you saying?' exclaims Pavel Alexandrovich.

'Imagine, my friend! I've been constantly taking you for the Vice-Governor, at the same time as thinking: why does he suddenly seem to have got a comple-tely di-fferent face?... The other one had such a, you know, stately, inte-lligent face. He was an ex-traor-dinarily intelligent man and was always compo-sing verse to mark various occasions. From the side, thus, he looked a little like the king of diamonds...'

'No, Prince,' Maria Alexandrovna interrupts, 'I swear you'll destroy yourself with such a life! Shutting yourself away for five years in solitude, seeing no one, hearing nothing! You're a lost man, Prince! Ask anyone you like from among those devoted to you, and they'll all tell you that you're a lost man!'

'Really?' exclaims the Prince.

'I assure you; I'm telling you as a friend, as your sister! I'm telling you because you're dear to me, because memories of the past are sacred for me! What advantage would there be for me in playing the hypocrite? No, you need to change your life fundamentally – otherwise you'll fall ill, you'll drain yourself, you'll die...'

'Oh, good heavens! Will I really die so soon?' exclaims the frightened Prince. 'And imagine, you've guessed right: I'm in extreme torment with my haemorrhoids, especially of late... And at the times when I have the attacks, the symptoms are, generally, a-sto-nishing (I'll describe them to you in the fullest detail)... Firstly...'

'Uncle, you can describe it another time,' Pavel Alexandrovich breaks in, 'but just now – isn't it time we were going?'

'Why yes! Another time, maybe. Perhaps it's not actually so inter-esting to listen to. I can see that now... But all the same, it's an extremely curious complaint. There are various episodes... Remind me, my friend, later this evening I'll tell you in de-tail about this one time...'

'But listen, Prince, you should try getting treatment abroad,' Maria Alexandrovna interrupts again.

'Abroad! Why yes, why yes! I shall go abroad without fail. I remember when I was abroad in the twenties it was a-ma-zing fun there. I almost married a viscountess, a Frenchwoman. I was extremely in love at the time and wanted to dedicate my whole life to her. However, it wasn't I who married her, but another. And what a strange thing: I was gone for only two hours, and another was triumphant, a German baron; later on, he was in the madhouse for a time as well.'

'But, *cher prince*, I was talking about the fact that you need to think seriously about your health. There are such physicians abroad... and besides, what is a change of lifestyle alone worth! You definitely need to abandon your Dukhanovo, at least for a time.'

'To be sure! I made my mind up long ago and, you know, I intend to have hy-dro-pa-thy treatment.'

'Hydropathy?'

'Hydropathy. I've already had hy-dro-pa-thy treatment once. I was at a spa at the time. There was a lady there from Moscow, I've forgotten her name now, but she was an extremely poetic woman, about seventy she was. Her daughter was with her too, about fifty, a widow, with a cataract in one eye. She practically spoke in verse as well. She had an a-ccident later on: she got angry and killed one of her serving-girls and stood trial for it. So they took it into their heads to give me water treatment. I confess, there was nothing the matter with me; well, but they badgered me: "Have the treatment, have the treatment!" Out of delicacy I did begin drinking the water; I'm thinking: I will indeed feel be-tter. I drank and drank, drank and drank, drank down a whole waterfall, and you know, this hydropathy is a beneficial thing and did me an awful lot of good, so that, if I hadn't finally fa-llen ill, I can assure you I'd have been perfectly well...'

'Now that is a perfectly fair conclusion, Uncle! Tell me, Uncle, have you studied logic?'

'Good heavens! The questions you ask!' the scandalised Maria Alexandrovna remarks sternly.

'I have, my friend, but a very long time ago. I learnt philosophy too, in Germany, I did the entire course, only I completely forgot everything there and then. But… I confess to you… you've frightened me so with these illnesses that I'm… all upset. However, I'll be back in a moment…'

'But where are you going, Prince?' cries the astonished Maria Alexandrovna.

'One moment, one moment… I'm just going to make a note of a new idea… *au revoir*…'

'What a man!' cries Pavel Alexandrovich, and bursts into roars of laughter.

Maria Alexandrovna loses her patience.

'I don't understand, I simply don't understand what you're laughing at!' she begins heatedly. 'Laughing at a venerable old man, a relative, laughing his every word to scorn, taking advantage of his angelic goodness! I've been blushing for you, Pavel Alexandrovich! But tell me, in what way is he ridiculous, in your view? I found nothing ridiculous about him.'

'The fact that he doesn't recognise people, the fact that he sometimes goes rambling on?'

'But it's a consequence of his terrible life, his terrible five-year imprisonment under the surveillance of that infernal woman. You should be feeling sorry for him, not laughing at him. He didn't even know me; you were yourself a witness. That in itself cries out, so to speak! He simply must be saved! I propose that he travel abroad, solely in the hope that he might abandon that… market trader!'

'Do you know what? We must find him a wife, Maria Alexandrovna!' exclaims Pavel Alexandrovich.

'Again! After this you're just incorrigible, Monsieur Mozglyakov!'

'No, Maria Alexandrovna, no! This time I'm being perfectly serious! Why not find him a wife? That's an idea too! *C'est une idée comme une autre*![22] Tell me, please, what harm can it do him? On the contrary, he's in such a position that a measure like that can only save him! By law, he can still marry. Firstly, he'll be delivered from that slyboots (forgive the expression). Secondly, and most importantly – imagine he chooses a girl or, even better, a widow, nice, kind, intelligent, gentle and, most importantly, poor, who will look after him like a daughter and understand he has done her a great favour in calling her his wife. And what can be better for him than a dear, a sincere and noble creature who will continually be beside him instead of that… peasant woman? It stands to reason, she has to be pretty, because to this day Uncle still likes pretty girls. Did you notice the way he couldn't take his eyes off Zinaida Afanasyevna?'

'And where ever will you find such a bride?' asks Nastasya Petrovna, who has been listening diligently.

'There you have it: why not you, if only you will! Permit me to ask: in what way are you not a fit bride for the Prince? Firstly – you're pretty, secondly – a widow, thirdly – noble, fourthly – poor (because you really aren't rich), fifthly – you're a very sensible lady, and consequently you'll love him, keep him in cotton wool, kick that madam out, take him abroad, you'll feed him semolina and sweets – all this until precisely the moment when he leaves this transient world, which will be in precisely a year, or perhaps even two and a half months. Then you're a princess, a widow, a rich woman and, in reward for your resolution, you'll marry a marquis or a quartermaster-general! *C'est joli*,[23] isn't it?'

'My word, good heavens! I think I'd fall in love with him, the dear, out of gratitude alone, if only he'd propose to me!' exclaims Mrs Zyablova, and her dark, expressive eyes begin to sparkle. 'Only it's all nonsense!'

'Nonsense? Do you want it not to be nonsense? Just ask me nicely, and then cut my finger off if you're not his fiancée this very day! There's nothing easier than persuading or enticing my uncle into something! He says "why yes, why yes" to everything – you've heard him yourself. We'll have him married and he won't even notice it. If you like, we'll have him married by deceiving him; but it's for his own good, after all, have some compassion!… You might at least smarten yourself up, Nastasya Petrovna, just in case!'

Monsieur Mozglyakov's enthusiasm is developing into positive fervour. No matter her sober-mindedness, Mrs Zyablova's mouth is, nonetheless, watering.

'I know I'm a perfect sloven today without being told by you,' she replies. 'I've let myself go completely – I stopped dreaming long ago. And the result's a Madame Gribousier[24] like this… What, do I really look like a cook?'

All this time Maria Alexandrovna has been sitting with a strange sort of expression on her face. I won't be mistaken if I say that she listened to Pavel Alexandrovich's strange proposition in a sort of fright, dumb-struck somehow… Finally she recovered herself.

'Let's suppose this is all very well and good, and yet it's all nonsense and absurdity, and, most importantly, utterly inopportune,' she abruptly cuts Mozglyakov short.

'But why, kindest Maria Alexandrovna, why is it nonsense and inopportune?'

'For a lot of reasons, but most importantly, because you are in my house, because the Prince is my guest, and because I won't allow anyone to forget to respect my house. I take your words for nothing more than a joke, Pavel Alexandrovich. But thank God, here's the Prince!'

'Here I am!' cries the Prince, entering the room. 'It's astonishing, *cher ami*, the number of different ideas I'm having today. And another time, perhaps you wouldn't even believe it, I don't seem to have any ideas at all. I just sit there the whole day.'

'It's probably because of your fall today, Uncle. It's shaken up your nerves, and so…'

'I ascribe it to that myself, my friend, and find this incident to have even been be-ne-fi-cial; so I've made up my mind to forgive my Feo-fil. You know what? I don't think he was making an attempt on my life; don't you think so? And besides, he was punished only recently anyway, when he had his beard shaved off.'

'His beard shaved off, Uncle! But doesn't he have a beard the size of Germany?'

'Well yes, it is the size of Germany. Generally speaking, my friend, you're absolutely right in your con-clu-sions. But the beard's a false one. And imagine, what a happy chance: suddenly I'm sent a pricelist. Newly received from abroad, the most splendid coachmen's and seigniorial beards, and, equally, side-whiskers, imperials, moustaches

34

and so on, and all this of the highest qua-lity and at the most reasonable prices. Why, I think, don't I send for a beard, to have a look at what it's like at least. And so I sent off for a coachman's beard – and the beard is, indeed, a wonder to behold! But it transpires that Feofil has his own, and it's almost twice the size. It stands to reason, a quandary arose: shave off his own one or send back the one that had been sent and wear the natural one? I thought and thought, and decided it was better to wear the artificial one.'

'No doubt because art is superior to nature, Uncle!'

'For that very reason. And the suffering it cost him when he was having his beard shaved! He parted with his beard as though parting with his whole career. But isn't it time for us to go, my dear?'

'I'm ready, Uncle.'

'But I do hope, Prince, you're going only to the Governor's!' exclaims Maria Alexandrovna in agitation. 'You're *mine* now, Prince, and you belong to my family for the whole day. Of course, I shan't say a thing to you about society here. Perhaps you'd like to visit Anna Nikolayevna, and I have no right to disenchant you: moreover, I'm quite certain that time will tell. But remember one thing, that I am your hostess, sister, wet-nurse, dry-nurse for the whole of today, and, I confess, I tremble for you, Prince! You don't know, no, you don't know these people fully, at least, you won't until the time comes!...'

'Depend upon me, Maria Alexandrovna. Everything will be as I promised you,' says Mozglyakov.

'Oh, you, you frivolous man! Depend upon you! I expect you for lunch, Prince. We have lunch early. And how I regret my husband being in the country on this occasion! How happy he would have been to see you! He respects you so, he's so sincerely fond of you!'

'Your husband? So you have a husband too?' asks the Prince.

'Oh, good heavens! How forgetful you are, Prince! You've completely, completely forgotten everything from before! My husband, Afanasy Matveyich, surely you remember him? He's in the country now, but you saw him a thousand times before. You remember, Prince: Afanasy Matveyich?...'

'Afanasy Matveyich! In the country, imagine, *mais c'est délicieux*! So you have a husband too? What a strange thing, though! It's like the vaudeville to the letter: *The Husband's off, and the Wife's in...* forgive me, I've gone and forgotten! Only the wife went somewhere too, Tula or Yaroslavl, in a word, it turns out very funny somehow.'

'*The Husband's off, and the Wife's in Tambov*, Uncle,' prompts Mozglyakov.[25]

'Ah-ha! That's it! Thank you, my friend, precisely, in Tambov, *charmant, charmant*! So it turns out smoothly as well. You're always in rhyme, my dear! Exactly, I remembered it: Yaroslavl or Kostroma, only the wife went somewhere too! *Charmant, charmant*! However, I've rather forgotten what I'd begun talking about... yes! And so, we're going, my friend. *Au revoir, madame, adieu, ma charmante demoiselle*,'[26] the Prince added, turning to Zina and kissing the tips of his fingers.

'For lunch, for lunch, Prince! Don't forget to come back quickly!' Maria Alexandrovna cries in his wake.

CHAPTER V

'You might look into the kitchen, Nastasya Petrovna,' she says, after seeing the Prince off. 'I have a feeling that fiend Nikitka is sure to go and spoil the lunch! I'm certain that he's already drunk…'

Nastasya Petrovna obeys. As she is leaving, she throws a suspicious glance at Maria Alexandrovna and notices an unusual sort of agitation about her. Instead of going to keep an eye on that fiend Nikitka, Nastasya Petrovna goes through into the reception hall, from there down the corridor to her own room, and from there into a little dark one, a small sort of lumber-room, where there are some chests standing about, various items of clothing hanging up, and where the dirty linen of the entire house is kept in bundles. On tiptoe she approaches a locked door, she stifles her breathing, bends down, looks through the keyhole and listens. This door is one of the three into that very room where Zina and her Mamma have now been left – always securely locked and nailed up.

Maria Alexandrovna considers Nastasya Petrovna a rather roguish, but extremely frivolous woman. Of course, it had sometimes occurred to her that Nastasya Petrovna wouldn't stand on ceremony even in respect of eavesdropping. But at the present moment Mrs Moskalyova is so preoccupied and agitated that she has completely forgotten about certain precautions. She sits down in an armchair and looks meaningfully at Zina. Zina feels this gaze upon her, and an unpleasant sort of melancholy starts pinching at her heart.

'Zina!'

Zina slowly turns her pale face towards her and raises her black, pensive eyes.

'Zina, I mean to have a talk with you about an extremely important matter.'

Zina turns round fully to face her Mamma, folds her arms and stands in expectation. In her face are annoyance and mockery, which she is, however, trying to conceal.

'I want to ask you, Zina, how *that* Mozglyakov seemed to you today?'

'You've already known for a long time what I think of him,' Zina replies reluctantly.

'Yes, *mon enfant*;[27] but it seems to me that he's becoming simply too persistent somehow with his… pursuit.'

'He says he's in love with me, and his persistence is excusable.'

'Strange! You didn't excuse him so… readily before. On the contrary, you always attacked him whenever I started talking about him.'

'It's strange too that you always used to defend him and wanted me to marry him without fail, but now you're the first to attack him.'

'Almost. I don't refuse to admit it, Zina: I wanted to see you married to Mozglyakov. It was hard for me to see your continual melancholy, your sufferings, which I am in a position to understand (whatever you might think of me!) and which poison my sleep at night. I finally felt convinced that only a significant change in your life could save you! And that change had to be marriage. We aren't rich, and we can't, for example, go abroad. The local asses are amazed that you're twenty-three and still not married, and they make up stories about it. But am I going to give you away to a local councillor, or to Ivan Ivanovich, our solicitor? Are there husbands for you here? Mozglyakov is shallow, of course, but he's better than the lot of them nonetheless. He's of respectable family, he has connections, he has a hundred and fifty souls; that's better, after all, than a life of deception and bribes and God knows what adventures; that's why I cast my gaze upon him. But I swear to you, I never had any genuine liking for him. I'm certain that the Almighty Himself was forewarning me. And if God were even now to send something better – oh, what a good thing it would be that you hadn't yet given him your word! You didn't say anything definite to him today, did you, Zina?'

'Why squirm so, Mamma, when the whole thing is said in just two words?' said Zina irritably.

'Squirm, Zina, squirm? How could you use such a word to your mother? But what am I saying! You haven't trusted your mother for a long time now! For a long time now you've considered me your enemy, not your mother!'

'Hey, enough, Mamma! Are we going to argue over a word? Don't we understand one another? I think we've had long enough!'

'But you insult me, my child! You don't believe that I'm ready to do absolutely anything, anything, to settle your fate!'

Zina glanced at her mother mockingly and with annoyance.

'You don't want to marry me off to the Prince, do you, to *settle* my fate?' she asked with a strange smile.

'I haven't said a word about it, but I might mention that if you did happen to marry the Prince, then it would be your good fortune and not folly...'

'And I think it's simply nonsense!' Zina exclaimed hot-temperedly. 'Nonsense! Nonsense! And I also think, Mamma, that you have too much poetic inspiration, you're a poetess in the full sense of the word; that's what they call you here. You're continually having projects. Their impossibility and foolishness doesn't deter you. I had a feeling while the Prince was still sitting here that you had this on your mind. When Mozglyakov was playing the fool and claiming that the old man had to be found a wife, I could read all your thoughts in your face. I'm prepared to bet you're thinking about it, and now you're approaching me with it. But since your continual projects concerning me are beginning to bore me to death, beginning to torment me, I'd ask you not to say a word to me about it, do you hear, Mamma – not a word, and I'd like you to remember it!' She was choking with rage.

'You're a child, Zina – an irritable, sick child!' replied Maria Alexandrovna in an emotional, tearful voice. 'You speak to me dis-respectfully and insult me. There's not a single mother would put up with what I put up with daily from you! But you're irritable, you're sick, you're suffering, and I'm a mother and, above all, a Christian. I must endure and forgive. But one word, Zina: if I really were dreaming of this union, why precisely do you consider it all nonsense? In my opinion, Mozglyakov never said anything wiser than he did just now, when he was arguing that marriage is essential for the Prince – not, of course, to that slattern Nastasya. There he got carried away.'

'Listen, Mamma! Tell me straight: are you asking this just out of curiosity, or with a purpose?'

'I'm simply asking: why does it seem to you such nonsense?'

'Oh, the irritation! I mean, why does a lot such as this have to fall to me!' Zina exclaims, stamping her foot in impatience. 'This is why, if you don't know it yet – not even to mention all the other absurdities: exploiting the fact that an old man has lost possession of his faculties, deceiving him, marrying him, a cripple, in order to pinch his money from him and then every day, every hour, wishing for his death, that, in my view, is not only nonsense but, what's more, so low, so low that I don't congratulate you on having such ideas, Mamma!'

The silence lasted about a minute.

'Zina! Do you remember what happened two years ago?' Maria Alexandrovna suddenly asked.

Zina winced.

'Mamma!' she said in a stern voice, 'you solemnly swore to me never to remind me of it.'

'And now I'm solemnly asking you, my child, to permit me just this once to break that promise, which I've never broken until now. Zina! The time has come for us to have everything out in full. These two years of silence have been dreadful! Things can't carry on like this!… I'm ready to beg you on my knees to permit me to speak. Do you hear, Zina: your own mother is imploring you on her knees! At the same time I give you my solemn word – the word of an unhappy mother who adores her daughter – that never, not on any account, not under any circumstances, even if it's a matter of saving my life, will I ever speak about it any more. This will be the last time, but now – it's essential!'

Maria Alexandrovna was counting on a big impact.

'Speak,' said Zina, noticeably paling.

'Thank you, Zina. Two years ago, there was a teacher coming to Mitya, your late little brother…'

'But why do you begin so solemnly, Mamma! Why all this eloquence, all these details, which are completely unnecessary, which are painful and which are all too well-known to both of us,' Zina cut her short with a sort of malicious repugnance.

'Because, my child, I, your mother, am now compelled to justify myself to you. Because I want to present this whole matter to you from a completely different point of view, and not from that erroneous one, from which you're accustomed to looking at it. And so that, finally, you might better understand the conclusion that I intend to draw from it all. Don't think, my child, that I want to play with your heart! No, Zina, you'll find in me a true mother, and, perhaps, as you melt into tears at my feet, at the feet of *a low woman*, as you've just called me, you will yourself beg for the reconciliation which you have for so long, so haughtily, until now been rejecting. That's why I want to say everything in full, Zina, everything from the very beginning; otherwise I remain silent!'

'Speak,' Zina repeated, cursing with all her heart her Mamma's need for eloquence.

'I continue, Zina: this teacher from the district college, still almost a boy, has an effect upon you that is completely incomprehensible to me. I was too reliant on your prudence, on your noble pride and, most importantly, on his worthlessness (because everything does need to be said) to suspect anything at all between you. And suddenly you come to me and resolutely announce that you intend to marry him! Zina! It was a dagger to my heart! I cried out and fainted away. But... you remember all that! It stands to reason, I considered it necessary to exercise all my power, which you called tyranny. Just think, a boy, the son of a sexton, receiving a salary of twelve roubles a month, a scribbler of lousy, wretched verse, which they publish out of pity in *The Library for Reading*,[28] and who can only talk about that damned Shakespeare – this boy is your husband, the husband of Zinaida Moskalyova! Why, it's worthy of Florian and his swains![29] Forgive me, Zina, but just the memory alone drives me out of my wits! I refused him, but no power can stop you. Your father, it stands to reason, just looked blank and didn't even understand what I'd begun explaining to him. You continue your relations, meetings even, with this boy, but what is most dreadful of all, you decide to correspond with him.

'Rumours are already beginning to spread through the town. People are beginning to taunt me with allusions; they're already rejoicing, they've started trumpeting the news far and wide, and suddenly all my predictions come true in the most triumphant manner. You quarrel over something; he proves the most unworthy... little boy (I'm quite unable to call him a man!) and threatens to distribute your letters around the town. At this threat, full of indignation, you lose your temper and give him a slap in the face. Yes, Zina, that fact too is known to me! Everything, everything is known to me!

'That same day, the wretch shows one of your letters to that scoundrel Zaushin, and an hour later the letter is already with Natalya Dmitriyevna, my mortal enemy. That same evening, in repentance, this madman makes an absurd attempt to poison himself with something. In short, the result is the most dreadful scandal! That slattern Nastasya comes running to me, alarmed, with terrible news: the letter has already been in Natalya Dmitriyevna's hands for a whole hour; in two hours the whole town will know of your disgrace! I mastered myself, I didn't fall into a faint – but with what blows did you strike my heart, Zina. That fiend, that shameless Nastasya demands two hundred silver roubles, and vows in return to get the letter back. I myself run in light shoes through the snow to Bumshtein the Jew and pawn my necklace – a memento of that righteous woman, my mother! Two hours later, the letter is in my hands. Nastasya has stolen it. She's broken open a casket and – your honour is saved, there's no evidence!

'But in what a state of alarm did you force me to live through that dreadful day! The very next day, for the first time in my life I noticed several grey hairs on my head. Zina! You yourself have now judged that boy's deeds. You yourself now agree, and perhaps with a bitter smile, that it would be the height of imprudence to entrust your fate to him. But ever since then you've been suffering, you've been in torment, my child; you can't forget him, or, to put it better, not him – he was always unworthy of you – but the spectre of your former happiness. That wretch is now on his deathbed; they say he has consumption, and you – an angel of goodness! – you don't want to marry in his lifetime, so as not to wound his heart, because to this day he is still racked with jealousy, although I'm sure he never loved you in a genuine, lofty way! I know that, on hearing of Mozglyakov's pursuit, he spied, sent in secret, pumped people. You're sparing him, my child, I've worked you out, and, as God's my witness, what bitter tears have I shed over my pillow!...'

'Oh, Mamma, drop it!' Zina cuts her short in inexpressible anguish. 'We really needed your pillow in all this,' she adds caustically. 'You can't do without declamation and affectation!'

'You don't believe me, Zina! Don't look at me with hostility, my child! My eyes haven't been dry these two years, but I've hidden my tears from you, and, I swear to you, I've changed in a lot of ways myself in this time! I came to understand your feelings long ago and, I'm sorry to say, have only now found out all the depth of your anguish. Can you blame me, my friend, for regarding this attachment as romanticism, brought upon you by that damned Shakespeare, who pokes his nose in as if on purpose everywhere he's not asked? What mother would condemn me for my fright back then, for the measures taken, for the severity of my judgement? But now, now, seeing you suffering for two years, I understand, I appreciate your feelings. Do believe that I've come to understand you perhaps much better than you understand yourself. I'm certain it's not him you love, that unnatural boy, but your own golden dreams, your lost happiness, your lofty ideals. I myself have loved, and perhaps more deeply than you. I myself have suffered; I too have had my lofty ideals. And therefore who can blame me now, and above all, can you blame me, for finding a union with the Prince the most salutary, the most essential thing for you in your current position?'

Zina had listened to the whole of this long declamation in surprise, knowing very well that her Mamma would never adopt such a tone without reason. But the final, unexpected conclusion utterly astonished her.

'So you really have seriously decided to marry me off to the Prince?' she exclaimed, looking in astonishment, almost in fright at her mother. 'And so it's not just dreams, not projects any longer, but your firm intention? So I've guessed it? And... and... how will this marriage save me, how is it essential in my present position? And... and... how does it all tie in with all the things you've just been saying – with that whole story?... I really don't understand you, Mamma!'

'And I'm amazed, *mon ange*,[30] at how it's possible to fail to understand it all!' exclaims Maria Alexandrovna, becoming animated in her turn. 'Firstly – the very fact alone that you move into a different society, into a different world! You leave behind for ever this repulsive, wretched little town, full of dreadful memories for you, where you have neither a kind word said to you, nor a friend, where you've been slandered, where all these magpies hate you for your beauty. You can even travel abroad this very spring, to Italy, to Switzerland, to Spain, Zina, to Spain, where there's the Alhambra, where there's the Guadalquivir, and not this place's horrid little river with its indecent name...'

'But permit me, Mamma, aren't you talking as though I'm already married, or at least as though the Prince has proposed to me?'

'Don't worry about that, my angel, I know what I'm saying. But allow me to continue. I've already said *the first thing*, now *the second thing*: I understand, my child, with what disgust you would give your hand to that Mozglyakov...'

'Even without your telling me, I know I shall never be his wife!' Zina replied with fervour, and her eyes began gleaming.

'And if only you knew how well I understand your disgust, my friend! It's a dreadful thing to vow love before God's altar for a man you cannot love! It's a dreadful thing to belong to a man you don't even respect! And he will demand your love; that's why he's marrying, I know that from the way he looks at you when you've turned away. How can I pretend? I've experienced it myself for twenty-five years. Your father ruined me. You might say he sucked all my youth out of me, and how many times have you seen my tears!...'

'Pappa's in the country, leave him be, please,' Zina replied.

'I know, you're his constant protectress. Oh, Zina! My heart would completely stop beating whenever I wished you to marry Mozglyakov for gain. But with the Prince there's no need for you to pretend. It goes without saying that you can't love him... with love, and he himself is *incapable* of demanding such love...'

'Good heavens, what nonsense! But I can assure you that you've been mistaken from the very beginning, about the very first, the main point! Know that I don't mean to sacrifice myself for who knows what! Know that I don't mean to marry at all, not anyone, and I shall remain a spinster! You've spent two years nagging me for not getting married. So, then – you'll have to reconcile yourself to it. I don't mean to, and that's that! That's the way it's going to be!'

'But Zinochka, darling, don't get heated, for God's sake, without hearing me out! And how hot-headed you are, truly! Allow me to look from my point of view, and you'll agree with me straight away. The Prince will live for a year, maximum two, and it's better to be a young widow, I think, than an overripe spinster, not even to mention the fact that after his death you're a princess, free, rich, independent! My friend, maybe you look with disdain upon all this calculating – calculating on his death! But – I'm a mother, and what mother would condemn me for being farsighted? Finally, if, angel of goodness, you still feel sorry for that boy, sorry to the extent that you don't even want to marry in his lifetime (as I guess), then just think that, by marrying the Prince, you'll force him to revive in spirit, to rejoice! If there's just one drop of common sense in him, then of course he'll realise that jealousy of the Prince is misplaced, ridiculous; he'll realise that you married for gain, out of necessity. Finally, he'll realise… that is, I just want to say that, after the Prince's death, you can marry again, anyone you like…'

'What emerges, quite simply, is this: marry the Prince, clean him out and then count on his death so as then to marry your lover. It's clever, the way you sum things up! You want to seduce me, suggesting I… I understand you, Mamma, I understand you completely! It's impossible for you to refrain from an exhibition of noble feelings, even in a matter like this. You'd do better to say it directly and simply: "Zina, it's a low trick, but it's profitable, and for that reason agree to it!" That would at least be more candid.'

'But why, my child, do you have to look from that point of view – from the point of view of deceit, treachery and cupidity? You take my calculations for baseness, for deceit? But for the sake of all that's holy, where's the deceit in it, what's base about it? Take a look at yourself in the mirror: you're so beautiful that a kingdom might be given in return for you! And suddenly, you – you, a beauty – you sacrifice your best years to an old man! Like a beautiful star, you light up the sunset of his life; like green ivy, you'll twine yourself around his old age, you, and not that stinging nettle, that vile woman who has bewitched him and is greedily sucking away his juices! Are his money and his princely title really worth more than you? So where are the deceit and the baseness here? You just don't know what you're saying, Zina!'

'They must be worth more, if I have to marry a cripple! Deceit is always deceit, Mamma, no matter what the aims might be.'

'On the contrary, my friend, on the contrary! It can even be looked at from an elevated, even from a Christian point of view, my child! You yourself once told me, in a kind of frenzy, that you wanted to be a sister of mercy. Your heart was suffering, it had become hardened. What you were saying (I know it) was that it was no longer able to love. If you don't believe in love, then direct your feelings towards a different, more lofty object, direct them sincerely, like a child, with all faith and sanctity, and God will bless you. That old man has suffered too, he is unhappy, he is persecuted; I've known him for several years now, and have always felt an incomprehensible liking for him, a kind of love, as if I had a presentiment of something. Be a friend to him, be a daughter to him, be, if you like, just a toy for him – if absolutely everything's to be said – but warm his heart, and you'll be doing it for God, for virtue!

'He's ridiculous – disregard that. He's only half a man – have pity on him: you're a Christian! Force yourself; such heroic deeds *are* forced. As we see it, bandaging wounds in a hospital is hard; breathing the infected air of an infirmary is repugnant. But there *are* angels of God who do all that and bless God for their purpose. Here you have a medicine for your insulted heart, a pursuit, a heroic deed – and you'll heal your own wounds. Where's the egotism in that, where's the mean trick in that? But you don't believe me! Perhaps you think I'm simulating when I talk about duty, about heroic deeds? Can't you understand that I, an empty society woman, can have a heart, feelings, principles? Well then, don't believe it, insult your mother, but do agree that her words are reasonable, salutary. Imagine, if you like, that it isn't me speaking, but someone else; close your eyes, turn towards the corner, imagine that it's some unseen voice talking to you… Is the main thing that's troubling you the idea it will all be for money, as though it's some kind of sale or purchase? Then you can always refuse the money, if the money is so hateful for you! Leave yourself just what is essential and distribute everything else to the poor. At least, for example, help *him*, that unfortunate, on his deathbed.'

'He won't accept any help,' said Zina quietly, as though to herself.

'*He* won't accept it, but his mother will,' replied the triumphant Maria Alexandrovna, 'keeping it quiet from him, she'll accept it. Six months ago you sold your earrings, a present from your aunt, and helped her; I know you did. I know the old woman washes other people's clothes to feed her unfortunate son.'

'He won't be needing any help soon!'

'I know that as well, what you're alluding to,' Maria Alexandrovna broke in, and inspiration, genuine inspiration came upon her, 'I know what you're speaking of. They say he's consumptive and will soon be dead. But who is it that's saying so? A few days ago I especially asked Kallist Stanislavich about him; I was taking an interest in him, because I do have a heart, Zina. Kallist Stanislavich replied that the illness is, of course, a dangerous one, yet that he's still sure the poor fellow isn't consumptive, but just has quite a serious chest disorder. Ask him yourself, if you like. He told me for certain that with different circumstances, especially with a change of climate and impressions, the patient could recover. He told me that in Spain – and I'd already heard this before, I'd even read about it – that in Spain there is some extraordinary island, Malaga,[31] I think – in short, like some sort of wine – where not only chest cases, but even genuine consumptives make complete recoveries thanks to the climate alone, and that people go there specially for treatment, only grandees, it stands to reason, or even, perhaps, merchants too, but only very rich ones. But that magical Alhambra alone, those myrtles, those lemon trees, those Spaniards on their mules! – all that alone would already make an extraordinary impression on a poetic nature.

'You think he won't accept your help, your money for the journey? Then deceive him, if you feel sorry for him! Deceit is pardonable for the salvation of a human life. Give him hope, promise him, finally, your love; say that you'll marry him once you're widowed. You can say absolutely anything at all in a noble way. Your mother won't teach you anything ignoble, Zina; you'll be doing this to save his life, and for that reason – everything is permissible! You'll revive him with hope; he'll start paying attention to his health himself, having treatment, listening to physicians. He'll try to revive for happiness. If he recovers, then even if you don't marry him – all the same he will have recovered, all the same you will have saved him, revived him! Even he can always be looked at with compassion! Perhaps fate has taught him a lesson and changed him for the better, and, if he really is worthy of you, maybe do marry him once you're widowed. You'll be rich, independent. Having cured him, you can give him a position in society, a career. Your marrying him will be more excusable then than now, when it's impossible.

'What awaits the two of you, if you were to resolve upon such madness now? Universal disdain, poverty, giving little boys a thick ear, because that's what his job entails, the shared reading of Shakespeare, an endless sojourn in Mordasov, and, finally, his imminent, inevitable death. Whereas by reviving him, you'll revive him for a useful life, for virtue; by forgiving him, you'll compel him to adore you. He's tormented by his vile action, but by opening up a new life to him, by forgiving him, you'll give him hope and reconcile him with himself. He can join the Civil Service, gain high rank. Finally, even if he doesn't recover, he'll die happy, reconciled with himself, in your arms – because you can be with him yourself in those moments – certain of your love, forgiven by you, beneath a canopy of myrtles and lemon trees, beneath an azure, exotic sky! Oh, Zina! It's all in your hands! All the advantages are with you – and it all comes via marriage to the Prince.'

Maria Alexandrovna stopped. Quite a long silence set in. Zina was inexpressibly agitated.

We don't undertake to describe Zina's feelings; we cannot divine them. But it seems that Maria Alexandrovna had found the genuine road to her heart. Not knowing what state her daughter's heart was now in, she had run through all those it might possibly be in, and finally guessed that she had come upon the right path. She had touched roughly upon all the most painful spots in Zina's heart and, it stands to reason, out of habit, had been unable to manage without an exhibition of noble feelings, which had not, of course, blinded Zina. 'But what does it matter that she doesn't trust me,' thought Maria Alexandrovna, 'if I can only make her stop and think! Only make subtle allusions to what I can't talk about directly!' This was what she had thought, and she had achieved her aim. The impact had been made. Zina had listened greedily. Her cheeks were burning, her breast heaving.

'Listen, Mamma,' she said resolutely at last, although the pallor that suddenly appeared on her face showed clearly what this resolution cost her. 'Listen, Mamma…'

But at that instant a sudden noise ringing out from the entrance hall and a sharp, strident voice asking for Maria Alexandrovna made Zina suddenly stop. Maria Alexandrovna leapt up from her seat.

'Oh, good heavens!' she exclaimed, 'what the devil brings that magpie, the Colonel's wife, here? I mean, I practically threw her out two weeks ago!' she added, almost in despair. 'But… but not to receive her now is impossible! Impossible! She must have brought news, otherwise she wouldn't have dared come. This is important, Zina! I need to know... Nothing should be disregarded now! But how grateful I am to you for your call!' she cried, rushing towards her guest as she came in. 'What made you think to remember me, my priceless Sofia Petrovna? What an en-chan-ting surprise!'

Zina ran from the room.

CHAPTER VI

The Colonel's wife, Sofia Petrovna Farpukhina, resembled a magpie only in terms of character. Physically, she rather resembled a sparrow. She was a small, fifty-year-old lady with sharp little eyes and with freckles and yellow blotches all over her face. On her dried-up little body, set on slender, strong, sparrow's legs, she had a dark, silk dress which was constantly rustling, because the Colonel's wife couldn't keep still for two seconds. She was a sinister and vindictive gossip. The fact that she was a colonel's wife had gone to her head. She very often fought with the retired Colonel, her husband, and scratched his face. Moreover, she drank four glasses of vodka in the morning and the same amount in the evening, and hated to distraction both Anna Nikolayevna Antipova, who had sent her packing from her house the previous week, and also Natalya Dmitriyevna Paskudina, who had assisted.

'I've come to see you just for a minute, *mon ange*,' she twittered. 'I've even sat down for no reason. I just dropped in to tell you what wonders are occurring here. The whole town has simply gone mad over the Prince! Our scoundrels – *vous comprenez!*[32] – are trying to catch him, searching for him, dragging him off one after the other, pouring champagne down him – you wouldn't believe it! Wouldn't believe it! What made you decide to let him go? Do you know that he's at Natalya Dmitriyevna's now?'

'Natalya Dmitriyevna's!' exclaimed Maria Alexandrovna, jerking up in her seat. 'But he was just going to the Governor's, and then, perhaps, to Anna Nikolayevna's, but even so, not for long!'

'Well, no, not for long; you try catching him now! He didn't find the Governor at home, then he went to Anna Nikolayevna's, promised to have lunch with her, and Natashka, who never leaves Anna Nikolayevna's now, she dragged him off to her place until then to have breakfast. And there's the Prince for you!'

'But what about… Mozglyakov? I mean, he promised…'

'You're obsessed with that vaunted Mozglyakov of yours… He went there with them too! See if they don't sit him down to play cards – he'll lose all his money again, like he did last year! And they'll sit the Prince down too; they'll take him to the cleaners. And the things she's putting around about you, that Natashka! She's shouting out loud that you're enticing the Prince, well… with certain ends – *vous comprenez*? She's talking to him about it herself. Of course, he doesn't understand anything, sits there like a wet cat, and to every word: "why yes! why yes!" And how about her, how about her! She wheeled out her Sonka – imagine: fifteen years old, and she still takes her around in a little short dress! It only comes down to her knees, you can imagine… That orphan Mashka was sent for, she's in a little short dress too, but above the knee even – I was looking through my lorgnette… They had plumed red hats of some kind sat on their heads – I have no idea what that means! – and the two little weeds were made to dance the kazachok in front of the Prince to a fortepiano accompaniment! Well, you know the Prince's weakness? He simply melted: "the forms," he says, "the forms!" He looks at them through his lorgnette, and they're excelling themselves, the two magpies! They've gone red in the face, they're twisting their legs about, and there's such *mon plaisir* being had that it's just hey nonny no! Pah! Call that a dance! I myself did a dance with a shawl when leaving Madame Jarny's Boarding School for Girls of the Nobility, and the effect produced was a noble one! I was applauded by senators! The daughters of princes and counts were educated there! But I mean, this was simply a can-can! I burnt up with shame, burnt up, burnt up! I simply couldn't sit through to the end!…'

'But… surely you weren't at Natalya Dmitriyevna's yourself? I mean, you…'

'Well yes, last week she insulted me. I tell everyone straight out. *Mais, ma chère*,[34] I felt an urge to take a look at the Prince, if only through a chink, and so I went. Where would I have seen him otherwise? Would I have gone to see her, if it hadn't been for that nasty wretch of a Prince! Imagine: everyone's served chocolate, but not me, and not one word was spoken to me in all that time. She was doing it on purpose, wasn't she… What an old bag! I'll let her have it now! But farewell, *mon ange*, I'm in a hurry now, in a hurry… I must be sure to catch Akulina Panfilovna in and tell her… But you can simply say goodbye to the Prince now! He won't be visiting you any more. He's got no memory, you know, so Anna Nikolayevna will be sure to drag him over to her place! They're continually afraid that you might… you understand? Regarding Zina…'

'*Quelle horreur!*'[35]

'That's what I'm telling you! The whole town's shouting about it. Anna Nikolayevna wants to be sure to keep him for lunch, and then for good. She's doing it to spite you, *mon ange*. I looked in through a chink at her yard. There was such a hullabaloo there: they're preparing lunch, knives are banging… they've sent for champagne. Hurry, hurry, and catch him on the way when he sets off for her place. After all, he promised to come to you for lunch first! He's your guest, not hers! To think of her laughing at you, that scoundrel, that player of dirty tricks, that whippersnapper! She's not worth the sole of my shoe, even if she is the Prosecutor's wife! I'm a colonel's wife myself! I was educated at Madame Jarny's Boarding School for Girls of the Nobility… Pah! *Mais adieu, mon ange!* I have my own sleigh, otherwise I'd go with you…'

The walking newspaper vanished, and Maria Alexandrovna started trembling with agitation, but the advice of the Colonel's wife was extremely clear and practical. There was no reason to delay, and no time either. Yet the chief difficulty still remained. Maria Alexandrovna rushed to Zina's room.

Zina was walking to and fro across the room with her arms folded and her head hanging, pale and upset. There were tears in her eyes; but in the gaze she directed at her mother there was the gleam of resolution. She hurriedly concealed the tears, and a sarcastic smile appeared on her lips.

'Mamma,' she said, forestalling Maria Alexandrovna, 'you've just spent a lot of your eloquence on me, too much. But you haven't blinded me. I'm not a child. Trying to convince yourself that I'm doing the heroic deed of a sister of mercy, without having the slightest vocation for it, trying to justify your base deeds, which you perform out of egotism alone, with noble ends – it's all such Jesuitry, and it couldn't deceive me. You hear: it couldn't deceive me, and I want you to be sure to know it!'

'But, *mon ange!*' cried the now timid Maria Alexandrovna.

'Be quiet, Mamma! Have the patience to hear me out in full. Despite being fully conscious of the fact that it's all just Jesuitry; despite my utter conviction that such an action is completely ignoble – I accept your proposal in full, do you hear: *in full*, and I declare to you that I'm prepared to marry the Prince, and am even prepared to assist all your efforts to make him marry me. Why am I doing this? You don't need to know. It's enough that I've resolved upon it. I've resolved upon everything: I'll hand him his boots, I'll be his housemaid, I'll dance for his pleasure, to make amends to him for my base deed; I'll do anything on earth so that he doesn't repent of having married me! But in return for my decision, I demand that you tell me candidly: how are you going to arrange it all? If you've begun talking about it so insistently, then – I know you – you couldn't have begun without having some definite plan in mind. Just for once in your life be candid; candour is an essential condition! I can't resolve upon it without actually knowing how you're going to do it all.'

Maria Alexandrovna was so taken aback by Zina's unexpected resolution that for some time she stood in front of her, dumb and motionless with astonishment, and gazed at her wide-eyed. Having prepared herself to do battle with the unyielding romanticism of her daughter, whose stern nobility constantly frightened her, she suddenly hears that her daughter is in complete agreement with her and is prepared to do anything, even contrary to her convictions! Consequently, the matter was taking on an extraordinary solidity – and joy began to sparkle in her eyes.

'Zinochka!' she exclaimed with enthusiasm, 'Zinochka! You're my flesh and blood!'

She could utter nothing more, and rushed to give her daughter a hug.

'Oh, good heavens! I'm not asking for your hugs, Mamma,' Zina exclaimed in impatient disgust, 'I don't need your raptures! I demand nothing more from you than a reply to my question.'

'But Zina, I mean, I love you! I adore you, and you push me away… I mean, it's for your happiness I'm trying…'

And unfeigned tears began shining in her eyes. Maria Alexandrovna really did love Zina, *in her own way*, and on this occasion, what with success and agitation, was extremely moved. Zina, despite certain limitations to her present view of things, understood that her mother loved her, and found that love oppressive. She would even have found it easier had her mother hated her…

'Come, don't be angry, Mamma, I'm so agitated,' she said, so as to calm her down.

'I'm not angry, I'm not angry, my little angel!' Maria Alexandrovna began twittering, becoming animated in an instant. 'I mean, I can understand that you're agitated. Now you see, my friend, you demand candour... all right, I'll be candid, completely candid, I assure you! If only you'd trust me. And firstly I'll tell you that a plan that's absolutely definite, that is to say, in every detail, is something I don't yet have, Zinochka, and cannot have; you, as a wise head, will understand why. I even foresee certain difficulties... Just now even, that magpie was jabbering all sorts of things to me... (Oh, good heavens! I need to hurry!) You see, I'm completely candid! But, I swear to you, I'll achieve the aim!' she added in rapture. 'My confidence is by no means poetry, as you were saying a little while ago, my angel; it's based on reality. It's based on the Prince's utter feeble-mindedness – and you know, that's a canvas on which you can embroider whatever you like. The most important thing is that people shouldn't interfere! And as to those fools outwitting me,' she exclaimed, banging her hand on the table with her eyes flashing, 'well, that's my affair! And the most essential thing of all in that respect is to get started as soon as possible, even to get all the most important things done today, if I possibly can.'

'Very well, Mamma, only hear out one more... *bit of candour*: do you know why I'm so interested in your plan and don't trust it? Because I can't count on myself. I've already said that I've resolved upon this base deed; but if the details of your plan are just too disgusting, too dirty, then I declare to you that I won't endure it and I'll give it all up. I know that's something else that's base: resolving upon something low and being afraid of the dirt it's swimming in, but what's to be done? That's the way it has to be!...'

'But Zinochka, what's especially low about this, *mon ange*?' Maria Alexandrovna timidly tried to object. 'It's just an advantageous marriage, and I mean, everyone does it! You just have to look from that viewpoint, and everything will seem very noble...'

'Oh, Mamma, for God's sake, don't try using cunning with me! You can see that I agree to everything, everything! So what more do you want? Please, don't be afraid if I call things by their proper names. Maybe that's my sole consolation now!'

And a bitter smile appeared on her lips.

'Well, well, all right, my little angel, we can be in disagreement in our minds and give one another mutual respect all the same. Only if you're worried about the details and are afraid that they'll be dirty, then leave all those concerns to me; I swear that not a drop of dirt will splash on you. Would I want to compromise you in front of everyone? Just rely on me, and everything will be settled most splendidly, most nobly, that's the main thing – most nobly! There'll be no scandal at all, and even if there is some kind of small, unavoidable little scandal – well... some kind of scandal – well, we'll already be far away by then, won't we? I mean, we won't stay here! Let them shout at the tops of their voices, to hell with them! They're the ones who'll be envious. And is it worth worrying about them? I'm even surprised at you, Zinochka (but don't get angry with me), how is it that you, with your pride, are afraid of them?'

'Ah, Mamma, I'm not afraid of them in the least! You don't understand me at all!' Zina answered irritably.

'Now, now, darling, don't get angry! I just mean to say that they themselves are playing dirty tricks every single day, and here you are just the one little time in your life... but silly me, what am I saying! It's not a dirty trick at all! Where's the dirty trick in it? On the contrary, it's even most noble. I'll prove it to you conclusively, Zinochka. Firstly, I repeat, it all depends on what point of view you look from...'

'Oh, enough of your proofs, Mamma!' cried Zina in anger, and stamped her foot impatiently.

'All right, darling, I'll stop, I'll stop! I forgot myself again...'

A short silence set in. Maria Alexandrovna followed Zina meekly and looked anxiously into her eyes, the way a little dog that has done something wrong looks into the eyes of its mistress.

'I don't even understand how you'll set about it,' Zina continued with disgust. 'I'm certain you'll run into nothing but shame. I despise their opinion, but for you it will be disgrace.'

'Oh, if that's all that's worrying you, my angel, then please, don't worry! I beg you, I implore you. If only we're in agreement, then don't worry about me. Oh, if you only knew the tight corners I've emerged from unscathed! I've had to handle things more difficult than this! Well, just let me have a go! In any event, first of all I need to be alone with the Prince as soon as possible. That's the very first thing! And everything else will depend on that! But I can foresee all the rest too. They'll all be up in arms, but... that's all right! I'll put them to shame myself! Mozglyakov worries me too...'

'Mozglyakov?' said Zina with disdain.

'Well yes, Mozglyakov; only don't be afraid, Zinochka! I swear to you that I'll get him to the point where he'll be helping us! You don't know me yet, Zinochka! You don't know yet what I'm like in action! Ah, Zinochka, darling, a little while ago, when I heard about the Prince, the idea began simply blazing in my head! It was as if all at once I'd been completely flooded with light. And who ever, who ever could have expected him to come to us? I mean, there won't be an opportunity like this in a thousand years! Zinochka, my little angel! There's no dishonour in marrying an old man and a cripple, it's in marrying someone you can't stand, and at the same time *truly* being his wife! Whereas you won't be a real wife to the Prince. It's not even a marriage, is it? It's simply a domestic contract! I mean, there'll be a benefit for him, the fool – the fool, he'll be given such inestimable happiness! Ah, what a beauty you are today, Zinochka! Not a beauty, but a super-beauty! I, if I were a man, I'd get you half a kingdom, if you wanted it! They're all asses! Now how can you resist kissing this little hand?' And Maria Alexandrovna gave her daughter's hand an ardent kiss. 'This is my body, my flesh, my blood, isn't it? He'll be married by force if necessary, the fool! And what a life you and I shall begin, Zinochka! You won't part with me, Zinochka, will you? You won't send your mother away when you meet with good fortune, will you? We may have argued, my little angel, but all the same, you've never had such a friend as me; all the same...'

'Mamma! If you really have resolved upon it, then perhaps it's time you... actually did something. You're just losing time here!' said Zina impatiently.

'It is time, it is, Zinochka, it is! Ah! I've been chattering on!' Maria Alexandrovna pulled herself up. 'That lot want to lure the Prince away for good. I'll be into my carriage and on my way at once! When I get there, I'll summon Mozglyakov, and then… Well, I'll carry him off by force, if necessary! Goodbye, Zinochka, goodbye, dear, don't grieve, don't doubt, don't be sad, the main thing is don't be sad! Everything will be managed beautifully, most nobly! The main thing is what viewpoint you look from… well, goodbye, goodbye!…'

Maria Alexandrovna made the sign of the cross over Zina, slipped out of the room, was busy in front of her mirror for a minute or so, and two minutes later was riding through the streets of Mordasov in her carriage on runners, made ready daily at about this hour in case she was going out. Maria Alexandrovna lived *en grand*.[36]

'No, you won't outwit me!' she thought, sitting in her carriage. 'Zina's agreed, so that means half the job's done, and grinding to a halt now – nonsense! Well done, Zina! Agreed in the end! So some little calculations have an effect on your head too! I presented her with an enticing prospect! Touched her! She's just so terribly pretty today! With her beauty, I'd have turned half of Europe upside down as I wanted! Well, we'll wait… Shakespeare'll go flying when she becomes a princess and gets to know something. What does she know? Mordasov and her teacher! Hm… Only what sort of princess will she be? I like that pride, that courage in her, how inaccessible she is! She throws a glance, and it's the glance of a queen! Now how, now how can you fail to understand your best interest! She's understood it at last! She'll understand the rest too… After all, I'll be with her, won't I! In the end she'll agree with me on every point! And she won't be able to do without me! I'll be a princess myself; I'll be recognised even in St Petersburg. Farewell, wretched little town! The Prince will die, that wretched boy will die, and then I'll marry her off to a foreign sovereign prince! There's one thing that worries me: did I confide in her too much? Was I too candid, was I too deeply moved? She worries me, oh, she worries me!'

And Maria Alexandrovna became lost in her thoughts. There's no denying it: they were restless. But it's said, isn't it, that a willing horse needs no spur.

Remaining alone, Zina walked to and fro across the room for a long time with her arms folded, deep in thought. She thought about many things. Often, and almost unconsciously she repeated: 'It's time, it's time, it's high time!' What did this fragmentary exclamation mean? More than once tears shone on her long, silky eyelashes. She didn't think of wiping them, of stopping them. But there was no reason for her Mamma to be worrying and trying to penetrate her daughter's thoughts: Zina had quite made up her mind and prepared herself for all the consequences…

'Hang on!' thought Nastasya Petrovna, making her way out of her lumber-room after the departure of the Colonel's wife. 'And there was I on the point of even wanting to pin a pink bow on for that wretched Prince! And I believed it, fool that I am, that he'd marry me! There's your bow for you! Ah, Maria Alexandrovna! You think I'm a slattern and a beggar, I take two-hundred-rouble bribes. But how could I let slip the chance of taking from you, you flashy creature, you! I took it in a noble way; I took for expenses connected with work… Perhaps I might have had to give someone a bribe myself! What is it to you that I didn't balk at breaking a lock with my own hands? It was for you I was working, you fine lady, you! All you want to do is embroidery on canvas! Just you wait, I'll show you a canvas. I'll show the two of you what a slattern I am! You'll find out about Nastasya Petrovna and all her meekness!'

CHAPTER VII

But Maria Alexandrovna was being borne away by her genius. She had conceived a great and bold plan. To marry her daughter off to a rich man, a prince and a cripple, to marry her off in secret from everyone, exploiting her guest's feeble-mindedness and defencelessness, to marry her off like a thief, as Maria Alexandrovna's enemies would say, was not merely bold, but even audacious. Of course, the plan had its benefits, but in the event of failure it covered its deviser in extraordinary shame. Maria Alexandrovna knew this, but didn't despair. 'I've emerged from tighter corners unscathed!' she had told Zina, and had done so with justice. What sort of a heroine would she otherwise be? It's indisputable that it was all rather like highway robbery; but Maria Alexandrovna paid no great attention to that either. In that regard she had a single, astonishingly accurate idea: 'Once they're married, they can't be unmarried' – a simple idea, but one which seduced the imagination with such extraordinary benefits that from just imagining those benefits Maria Alexandrovna was all aquiver and tingling. She was dreadfully agitated generally, and sat in her carriage as though on tenterhooks. As an inspired woman, gifted with undoubted creativity, she had already managed to create a plan of action. But this plan was drawn up in rough, in general terms, *en grand*, and was still somehow visible to her only dimly. Ahead lay a host of details and various unforeseen circumstances. But Maria Alexandrovna had confidence in herself: she was agitated not with fear of failure – no! She just wanted to get started quickly, to go into battle quickly. Impatience, noble impatience burnt her up at the thought of delays and stops.

But, having mentioned delays, we beg leave to elucidate our idea somewhat. Maria Alexandrovna foresaw and expected the greatest trouble from her noble fellow citizens, the Mordasovans, and primarily from the noble society of Mordasov's ladies. She knew from experience all their irreconcilable hatred for her. She knew for sure, for example, that people in the town might already at the present time know all her intentions, although no one had yet told anyone about them. She knew from repeated sad experience that there was no event in her house, not even the most secret, that, having taken place in the morning, would not already be known by the evening to the last tradeswoman at the market, to the last salesman in the shop. Of course, Maria Alexandrovna still had only presentiments of trouble, but such presentiments never deceived her. Neither was she deceived now. This is what had actually happened, and what she did not yet positively know.

At around noon, that is to say, exactly three hours after the Prince's arrival in Mordasov, strange rumours had spread through the town. Where they began is unknown, but they went round almost instantly. All suddenly began asserting to one another that Maria Alexandrovna had already promised her Zina to the Prince, her twenty-three-year-old Zina with no dowry; that Mozglyakov had been dismissed, and that everything was already signed and sealed. What was the reason for such rumours? Did everyone really know Maria Alexandrovna to such an extent that they had got right to the heart of her cherished thoughts and ideals at once? Neither the incompatibility of this rumour with the usual order of things – because such matters can very rarely be arranged in an hour – nor the apparent unfoundedness of this piece of news – because no one could find out where it had originated – could undermine the Mordasovans' faith. The rumour grew and took root with extraordinary persistence. Most astonishing of all is that it had started to spread at precisely the time when Maria Alexandrovna had set about the conversation she had just had with Zina on that very subject. Such is the sensitivity of provincial folk! The instinct of provincial newsmongers sometimes reaches a miraculous level and, of course, there are reasons for this. It is based on their most intimate and interesting study of one another, conducted over many years. Every provincial person lives as though under a bell-jar. There is absolutely no chance of concealing anything at all from your estimable fellow-citizens. People know you off by heart, they know even what you don't know about your own self. One would think that the provincial person ought, by his very nature, to be a psychologist and reader of the human heart. That's why I have sometimes been sincerely surprised when very often encountering in the provinces not psychologists and readers of the human heart, but extremely large numbers of asses instead. No more of that, though; it's a superfluous idea. The news was thunderous. Marriage to the Prince seemed to everyone so advantageous, so brilliant, that even the strange side of the matter failed to arrest anyone's attention.

We shall note one more fact: Zina was hated almost even more than Maria Alexandrovna – why is unknown. Perhaps Zina's beauty was in part the reason for it. Perhaps the fact too that for all Mordasovans Maria Alexandrovna was, after all, somehow one of their own, *cast in the same mould*. If she disappeared from the town – who knows? – perhaps she would be missed. She enlivened society with continual incidents. It would be dull without her. Zina, on the contrary, conducted herself as though she lived in the clouds and not in the town of Mordasov. She was not a good match for these people somehow, not right for them, and, perhaps without noticing it herself, she behaved with intolerable haughtiness before them.

And now suddenly this same Zina, about whom there were even some scandalous stories, this haughty, this proud Zina is to become a millionaire, a princess, is to join the aristocracy. In a couple of years, when she is widowed, she'll marry some duke or other, maybe even a general; what's more, for all one knows, perhaps a governor (and as luck would have it, the Governor of Mordasov is a widower and extremely tender towards the female sex). Then she'll be the first lady in the Province, and, it stands to reason, that idea alone was intolerable in itself, and there was no news that would ever have aroused such indignation in Mordasov as the news about Zina marrying the Prince. Furious cries instantly rose up on all sides. People cried that it was sinful, even ignoble; that the old man wasn't in his right mind; that the old man had been deceived, duped, bamboozled by people exploiting his feeble-mindedness; that the old man had to be saved from bloodthirsty claws; that, ultimately, it was robbery and immorality; ultimately, in what way were other people worse than Zina? And other people might have married the Prince in exactly the same way.

All this talk, these exclamations were still only Maria Alexandrovna's assumptions, but that was enough for her. She knew for sure that everyone, absolutely everyone would be ready to employ all possible means and even impossible means to obstruct her intentions. They wanted to confiscate the Prince now, didn't they, and so he had to be got back, practically by force. Ultimately, even if she were successful in catching the Prince and enticing him back, it wouldn't be possible to keep him on a leash for ever. Ultimately, who could guarantee that the entire solemn choir of Mordasov's ladies would not today, in just two hours' time, be in her salon, and on such a pretext, what's more, that it would be impossible to refuse them? Refuse them the door and they'd come in through the window: an almost impossible thing to happen, but one which *had* happened in Mordasov. In short, not an hour, not a bit of time was to be lost, and yet things still hadn't even been started.

Suddenly, a brilliant idea flashed through Maria Alexandrovna's mind and instantly matured. We shall not forget to say something about this new idea in the appropriate place. For now we shall say only that at that moment our heroine was flying through the streets of Mordasov, awesome and inspired, resolved even upon a genuine fight, if the necessity only arose, to regain possession of the Prince. She didn't yet know how this would be done or where she would meet him, but she did, on the other hand, know for certain that Mordasov was more likely to be swallowed up by the earth, than was even one iota of her present plans to be unfulfilled.

The first step could not have been more successful. She managed to intercept the Prince in the street and took him home for lunch. If I'm asked how, in spite of all her enemies' machinations, she nonetheless succeeded in having things her own way and leaving Anna Nikolayevna with her nose really rather out of joint, then I'm obliged to declare that I even consider such a question an insult to Maria Alexandrovna. Will she fail to carry the day against some Anna Nikolayevna Antipova? She simply arrested the Prince as he was already driving up to her rival's house, and, regardless of everything, and regardless too of the arguments of Mozglyakov himself, who was afraid of a scandal, she made the old man get into her carriage. The way Maria Alexandrovna differed from her rivals was that in decisive circumstances she didn't stop to think even in the face of scandal, taking it as axiomatic that success justifies anything. It stands to reason, the Prince offered no significant resistance and, as was his wont, very quickly forgot about everything and was most content. At lunch he chattered incessantly and was extremely cheerful, cracking jokes, making puns, relating anecdotes and failing to finish them or skipping from one to another without noticing it himself. At Natalya Dmitriyevna's he had drunk three glasses of champagne. At lunch he drank some more and got into a complete spin. It was Maria Alexandrovna herself filling his glass now. Lunch was very respectable. That fiend Nikitka didn't mess things up. The hostess enlivened the company with the most charming courtesy. But the others who were present were, as if on purpose, extraordinarily miserable. Zina was somehow solemnly taciturn. Mozglyakov was evidently ill at ease and ate little. He was thinking about something, and since this was quite rarely the case with him, Maria Alexandrovna was greatly disquieted. Nastasya Petrovna sat gloomily, and even made some strange, stealthy signs to Mozglyakov, which the latter completely failed to notice. Had it not been for the charmingly courteous hostess, lunch would have been like a funeral.

Yet at the same time, Maria Alexandrovna was inexpressibly agitated. Zina alone was already worrying her dreadfully with her sad air and tear-stained eyes. And here was another difficulty too: she needed to hurry, to make haste, but 'that damned Mozglyakov' was sitting there like a blockhead with nothing to worry him and just being a hindrance! After all, you really couldn't start something like this in front of him! Maria Alexandrovna rose from the table in terrible disquiet. What, then, was her astonishment, her joyous fright, if one can express it so, when, as soon as they had risen from the table, Mozglyakov came up to her himself and suddenly, quite unexpectedly, declared that – to his deepest regret, it stands to reason – it was essential for him to leave at once.

'To go where?' Maria Alexandrovna asked with extraordinary commiseration.

'You see, Maria Alexandrovna,' Mozglyakov began in disquiet, even getting somewhat flustered, 'a very strange thing has happened to me. I really don't know how to tell you... for God's sake, give me your advice!'

'What, what is it?'

'My godfather, Boroduyev, you know – the merchant... met with me today. The old man's really angry, reproachful, tells me I've become stuck-up. Here I am in Mordasov a third time, and I've not even shown my face at his house. "Come to tea," he says, "today." It's exactly four o'clock now, and he takes tea, like in the olden days, as soon as he wakes up after four. What am I to do? It's obvious, Maria Alexandrovna – but just think! I mean, he saved my late father from the noose when he'd been gambling away public money. That was the reason why he christened me. If my marriage to Zinaida Afanasyevna takes place, I only have a hundred and fifty souls, after all. But he's got a million roubles, you know, even more, people say. He's childless. If you get on his right side – he'll leave you a hundred thousand in his will. Seventy years old – just think!'

'Oh, good heavens! So what are you doing? Why are you lingering?' exclaimed Maria Alexandrovna, scarcely concealing her joy. 'Go, go! This isn't to be taken lightly. I could see there was something, you were so miserable at lunch! Go, *mon ami*, go! You should have paid him a visit this morning, shown that you value, that you appreciate his kindness! Ah, youngsters, youngsters!'

'But I mean, you yourself, Maria Alexandrovna,' exclaimed Mozglyakov in amazement, 'you yourself used to attack me over this acquaintanceship! Didn't you say he was a bearded peasant, a relative of taverners, vodka-cellar keepers and attorneys?'

'Ah, *mon ami*! Don't we say all manner of ill-considered things? I can make mistakes too, I'm no saint. Anyway, I don't remember, but I may have been in such a frame of mind… And in the end, you weren't yet courting Zinochka then… Of course it's egotism on my part, but now, like it or not, I have to look at things from a different point of view and – what mother can blame me in this instance? Go, don't linger for a moment! Stay the evening with him even… and listen! Find a way to talk to him about me. Say that I respect, love, honour him, and do it really cleverly, really well! Ah, good heavens! And it had gone right out of my head, you know! I should have thought of giving you the idea myself!'

'You've revived me, Maria Alexandrovna!' exclaimed the admiring Mozglyakov. 'I swear, I'm going to listen to you in everything now! I was just afraid of telling you, you see!… Well, goodbye, I'm on my way! Make my excuses to Zinaida Afanasyevna. However, I'll be here without fail…'

'My blessing, *mon ami*! Mind you do have a talk with him about me! He really is a very nice old man. I changed my ideas about him long ago… And I always did, incidentally, like all that genuine old-time Russianness about him… *Au revoir, mon ami, au revoir*!'

'What a good thing that the Devil's got into him! No, this is God Himself helping out!' she thought, breathless with joy.

Pavel Alexandrovich went out into the entrance hall and was already putting on his fur coat when suddenly, from out of nowhere, there was Nastasya Petrovna. She had been lying in wait for him.

'Where are you going?' she said, holding him back by the arm.

'To Boroduyev's, Nastasya Petrovna! My godfather; he did me the honour of christening me… He's a rich old man and he's going to leave me something, I need to flatter him a bit!…'

Pavel Alexandrovich was in the most excellent frame of mind.

'To Boroduyev's! Well, say goodbye to your bride then,' said Nastasya Petrovna abruptly.

'What do you mean, "say goodbye"?'

'What I said! You thought she was already yours! But here they are wanting to marry her off to the Prince. I heard it myself!'

'To the Prince? For pity's sake, Nastasya Petrovna!'

'Why "for pity's sake"? Would you like to look and listen for yourself? Just drop the coat and come this way!'

The stupefied Pavel Alexandrovich dropped his fur coat and set off on tiptoe after Nastasya Petrovna. She led him to that same lumber-room from which she had spied and eavesdropped in the morning.

'But pardon me, Nastasya Petrovna, I don't understand an absolute thing!…'

'But you will when you bend down and listen. The comedy will doubtless be starting any minute now.'

'What comedy?'

'Ssh! Don't talk so loud! The comedy is that you're simply being duped. Earlier on, when you'd left with the Prince, Maria Alexandrovna spent a whole hour persuading Zina to marry him, saying there was nothing easier than bamboozling him and making him get married, and wheeling out such deceit that it even made me feel sick. I heard everything from here. Zina consented. The way the two of them were slating you! They simply take you for a fool, and Zina said outright that she wouldn't marry you for anything. I'm an idiot! Wanted to pin a red bow on! Just listen, listen!'

'But I mean, it's the most outrageous treachery, if that's so!' whispered Pavel Alexandrovich, looking into Nastasya Petrovna's eyes in the silliest way.

'Just you listen, and that's not all you'll hear.'

'But where do I listen?'

'Just bend down, through this little hole here…'

'But Nastasya Petrovna, I'm… I'm not capable of eavesdropping.'

'And when did you get that idea! Pocket your honour here, my dear fellow; there they are now, so listen!'

'But all the same…'

'If you're not capable, then you can be left looking foolish! Someone feels sorry for you, and here you are showing off! What's it to me? I'm not doing it for myself, you know. I won't even be here come this evening!'

Pavel Alexandrovich bent down reluctantly to the chink. His heart was pounding, there was a thumping in his temples. He scarcely understood what was happening to him.

CHAPTER VIII

'So you had a really jolly time at Natalya Dmitriyevna's, Prince?' asked Maria Alexandrovna, casting a rapacious glance over the field of the forthcoming battle and wanting to begin the conversation in the most innocent manner. Her heart was pounding with excitement and expectation.

Immediately after lunch the Prince had been led into 'the salon' in which he had been received that morning. All ceremonial events and receptions at Maria Alexandrovna's took place in that same salon. She was proud of the room. After six glasses the old man had gone quite limp somehow and was rather unsteady on his legs. And yet he chattered incessantly. His chattering had even increased. Maria Alexandrovna understood that this was a momentary outburst, and that her guest, heavy with the meal, would soon want a sleep. The moment had to be seized. Surveying the field of battle, she noticed with delight that the voluptuous old man was throwing glances at Zina that were somehow particularly lascivious, and her parental heart began to quiver with joy.

'Ex-treme-ly jolly,' the Prince replied, 'and, you know, she's the most in-com-pa-rable woman, Natalya Dmitriyevna, the most in-com-parable woman.'

No matter how preoccupied Maria Alexandrovna was with her great plans, such resounding praise for her rival pricked her right in the heart.

'Pardon me, Prince!' she exclaimed, with her eyes flashing, 'but if your Natalya Dmitriyevna's an incomparable woman, then I really don't know what's going to come after that! You really don't know society here at all after that, you don't know it at all! I mean, it's just an exhibition of one's unprecedented virtues, one's noble feelings, just a comedy, just a golden outer crust. Raise the crust a little and you'll see a whole hell underneath the flowers, a whole hornet's nest, where they'll eat you up and not leave the bones!'

'Surely not?' exclaimed the Prince. 'I'm amazed!'

'But I swear to you it's so! *Ah, mon prince*! Listen, Zina, I must, it's my duty to tell the Prince about the ridiculous and base thing that happened with that Natalya last week – do you remember? Yes, Prince – it's about that very same, vaunted Natalya Dmitriyevna of yours, whom you admire so much. Oh, my dearest Prince! I swear, I'm not a gossip! But I shall certainly tell you this, solely to make you laugh, to show you with a live specimen, so to speak, through an optical glass, what people here are like! Two weeks ago this Natalya Dmitriyevna comes to see me. Coffee was served, and I left the room to fetch something. I remember very well how much sugar I'd left in the silver sugar-bowl: it was completely full. I come back and look: lying on the bottom of it there are just three lumps. No one apart from Natalya Dmitriyevna had been left in the room. How about that woman! She has her own stone house and countless sums of money! It's a ridiculous incident, comic, but make your judgement of society here after that!'

'Sure-ly not!' the Prince exclaimed, sincerely amazed. 'But what unnatural greed! Surely she didn't eat it all by herself?'

'Well, that's what a *most incomparable* woman she is, Prince! How do you like such a shameful incident? I think I would have died at the very same moment I resolved upon such a disgusting deed!'

'Why yes, yes… Only, you know, she's such a *belle femme*[37] all the same…'

'Natalya Dmitriyevna! Pardon me, Prince, but she's simply an old bag! Ah, Prince, Prince! What have you said! I expected much greater taste from you…'

'Why yes, an old bag… only, you know, she's so well-formed… Well, and that girl who was dan-cing, she too is… well-formed…'

'Sonyechka? But I mean, she's still a child, Prince! She's only fourteen years old!'

'Why yes… only, you know, she's so nimble, and she has… such forms too… forming. So sweet! And the other one who was dan-cing with her, she too is… forming…'

'Ah, she's an unfortunate orphan, Prince! They often have her there.'

'An or-phan. Dirty, though, she might at least have washed her hands… But al-lur-ing too, though…'

As he was saying this, the Prince was examining Zina through his lorgnette with a sort of growing greed.

'*Mais quelle charmante personne!*'[38] he muttered under his breath, melting with delight.

'Zina, play something for us, or no, better sing something! How she sings, Prince! She's a virtuoso, you might say, a genuine virtuoso! And if only you knew, Prince,' Maria Alexandrovna continued in a low voice, when Zina had gone over to the grand piano, walking with her soft, gliding tread, which all but made the poor old man double up, 'if only you knew what a daughter she is! The way she knows how to love, how tender she is with me! What feelings, what a heart!'

'Why yes… feelings… and do you know, I've only known one woman in all my life with whom she could compare in bea-uty,' the Prince interrupted, swallowing down his saliva. 'It's the late Countess Nayinskaya, she died about thirty years ago. She was a ra-vi-shing woman of indescri-bable beauty, and then she went and married her cook…'

'Her cook, Prince?'

'Why yes, her cook… a Frenchman, abroad. She got him the title of count abro-ad. He was a fine figure of a man, and extremely well-educated, with this little mous-tache.'

'And, and… how did they get on, Prince?'

'Why yes, they got on well. However, they soon parted afterwards. He cleaned her out and left. They quarrelled over some kind of sauce…'

'Mamma, what should I play?' asked Zina.

'Better if you sang for us, Zina. How she sings, Prince! Are you fond of music?'

'Oh yes! *Charmant, charmant*! I'm very fond of mu-sic. I was acquainted with Beethoven when abroad.'

'Beethoven! Imagine, Zina, the Prince was acquainted with Beethoven!' Maria Alexandrovna cries in delight. 'Oh Prince! Were you really acquainted with Beethoven?'

'Why yes… he and I were on a friend-ly foo-ting. And his nose was forever covered in snuff. Such a funny man!'

'Beethoven?'

'Why yes, Beethoven. Though perhaps it wasn't Beet-ho-ven, but some other Ger-man. There are a great number of Ger-mans there… However, I seem to be getting muddled.'

'So what shall I sing, Mamma?' asked Zina.

'Ah, Zina! Sing that romance where, you remember, there's a lot of chivalry, where there's that mistress of a castle and her troubadour too... Ah, Prince! How I love all that chivalry! Those castles, castles!... That medieval life! Those troubadours, heralds, tournaments... I'll accompany you, Zina. Move to this seat, Prince, a little closer! Ah, those castles, castles!'

'Why yes... castles. I like ca-stles too,' the Prince mumbles in rapture, with his one eye fastened upon Zina. 'But... good heavens!' he exclaims, 'it's that romance!... I know that romance! I heard that romance long ago... It so re-minds me... Ah, good heavens!'

I don't undertake to describe what came over the Prince when Zina started to sing. She sang an old French romance that had once been the height of fashion. Zina sang it beautifully. Her pure, sonorous contralto pierced to the heart. Her beautiful face, her wonderful eyes, the marvellous, finely moulded fingers with which she turned the music, her hair, thick, black and shiny, her heaving breast, her entire figure, proud, beautiful, noble – all of it bewitched the poor old man completely. He couldn't take his eyes off her as she sang, he was transported with excitement. His old man's heart, heated up by the champagne, by the music and by the memories revived (and who does not have memories they love?), thumped ever more rapidly, in a way it had not beaten for a long time... He was ready to drop to his knees before Zina, and was almost crying when she finished.

'*O ma charmante enfant!*' he exclaimed, kissing her fingers. '*Vous me ravissez!*[39] Only now, now have I remembered... But... but... *o ma charmante enfant...*'

And the Prince couldn't even finish.

Maria Alexandrovna sensed that her moment had come.

'Why are you destroying yourself, Prince?' she exclaimed solemnly. 'So much feeling, so much vitality, so much spiritual wealth, and burying yourself in isolation for the rest of your life! Running away from people, from friends! Why, it's unforgivable! Think again, Prince! Look at life, so to speak, with a clear eye! Call up from your heart memories of the past – memories of your golden youth, of golden, carefree days – resurrect them, resurrect yourself! Start to live in society again, amongst people! Go abroad, to Italy, to Spain – to Spain, Prince!... You need a guide, a heart to love and respect you, to feel for you? But you have friends! Summon them, call them, and they'll come running in droves! I'll be the first to abandon everything and come running at your call. I remember your friendship, Prince; I'll abandon my husband and follow you... and if I were still younger, if I were as fine and beautiful as my daughter, I would even become your companion and helpmate, your wife, if that were what you wanted!'

'And I'm sure you were *une charmante personne* in your day,' said the Prince, blowing his nose into a handkerchief. His eyes were wet with tears.

'We live in our children, Prince,' Maria Alexandrovna replied with high emotion. 'I too have my guardian angel! And this is her, my daughter, the friend of my thoughts, of my heart, Prince! She's already turned down seven proposals, not wishing to part with me.'

'And so she'll come with you when you ac-com-pany me a-broad? In that case I shall definitely go abroad!' exclaimed the Prince, becoming animated. 'I shall de-fin-itely go! And if I could flatter myself with the hope... But she's an enchanting, en-chan-ting child! *O ma charmante enfant!*...' And the Prince began kissing her hands once more. The poor thing, he wanted to kneel down before her.

'But... but Prince, you say: can you flatter yourself with hope?' Maria Alexandrovna picked up on his words, sensing a new surge of eloquence. 'Now you're a strange man, Prince! Do you really consider yourself no longer worthy of the attention of women? It isn't youth that constitutes beauty. Remember that you are, so to speak, a fragment of the aristocracy! You're a representative of the most refined, the most chivalrous feelings and... manners! Did Maria not fall in love with old Mazepa?[40] I remember I read that Lauzun, that enchanting Marquis at the court of Louis...[41] I've forgotten which one, when already in declining years, already an old man, conquered the heart of one of the leading court beauties!... And who told you you were an old man? Who taught you that? Do people like you really grow old? You have such a wealth of feelings, ideas, gaiety, wit, vitality, brilliant manners! And if you appear somewhere now, abroad, at a spa, with a young wife, with just such a beauty as, for example, my Zina – I'm not talking about her, I'm saying it just for comparison – you'll see what a colossal impact there'll be! You – a fragment of the aristocracy, she – a beauty of beauties! You lead her solemnly by the arm; she sings in brilliant society, you, for your part, pour forth your wit – and the whole spa will gather to look at you! The whole of Europe will cry out, because all the newspapers, all the feuilletons at the spa will speak out in a single voice... Prince, Prince! And you say: can you flatter yourself with hope?'

'The feuilletons... why yes, why yes!... They're in the newspapers...' mutters the Prince, not understanding half of Maria Alexandrovna's chatter, and becoming more and more limp. 'But... my child, if you're not tired, repeat that romance you just sang one more time!'

'Ah, Prince! But she has other romances too, even better ones... Do you remember "*L'hirondelle*", Prince?[42] You must have heard it?'

'Yes, I do remember it... or to put it better, I've for-gotten it. No, no, the earlier ro-mance, the one that she sang just now! I don't want "*L'hirondelle*"! I want that romance...' said the Prince, beseeching like a child.

Zina sang it again. The Prince couldn't contain himself and dropped to his knees before her. He was crying.

'*O ma belle châtelaine!*'[43] he exclaimed, and his voice jangled with old age and excitement. '*O ma charmante châtelaine!* Oh, my dear child! You have re-min-ded me of so much... of what is long past... I thought then that everything would be better than it subsequently was. I sang duets then... with the Viscountess... that very romance... but now... Now I don't know what...'

The Prince delivered this entire speech panting and choking. His tongue had noticeably stiffened. It was almost completely impossible to make out some of the words. It was clear only that he felt moved in the highest degree. Maria Alexandrovna immediately poured oil onto the fire.

'Prince! Why, you're quite likely going to fall in love with my Zina!' she exclaimed, sensing that the moment was a solemn one.

The Prince's reply exceeded her best expectations.

'I am madly in love with her!' the old man exclaimed, suddenly becoming all animated, still kneeling and all atremble with excitement.

74

'I'm ready to give her my life! And if I could only hope... But help me up, I'm a little weak... I... if I could only hope to offer her my heart, then... I... she would sing me ro-man-ces every day, and I would just keep looking at her... just keep looking... Ah, good heavens!'

'Prince, Prince! You're offering her your hand! You want to take her from me, my Zina! My dear, my angel, Zina! But I won't let you go, Zina! Let them tear her from my arms, from the arms of her mother!' Maria Alexandrovna rushed to her daughter and squeezed her tight in her embrace, even though she felt she was being quite firmly pushed away... Mamma was overdoing it a little. Zina felt it with the whole of her being, and was watching this entire comedy with inexpressible disgust. She was, however, silent, and that was all Maria Alexandrovna required.

'She refused nine times just so as not to part with her mother!' she cried. 'But now – my heart has a presentiment of parting. I'd already noticed before that she was looking at you so... You have smitten her, Prince, with your aristocratic ways, that refinement!... Oh, you will part us; I have a presentiment of it!...'

'I a-dore her!' mumbled the Prince, still trembling like an aspen leaf.

'And so, you are abandoning your mother!' exclaimed Maria Alexandrovna, throwing herself once more onto her daughter's neck.

Zina hastened to end this trying scene. In silence she reached out her beautiful hand to the Prince and even forced herself to smile. The Prince took the little hand reverentially and covered it in kisses.

'Only now do I be-gin to live,' he mumbled, transported with delight.

'Zina!' said Maria Alexandrovna solemnly, 'look at this man! This is the most honourable, the noblest of all the men I know! This is a knight of the Middle Ages! But she knows it, Prince; she knows, to the sorrow of my heart... Oh, why did you come! I hand her over to you, my treasure, my angel. Take care of her, Prince! It's a mother who implores you, and what mother would condemn me for my grief?'

'Mamma, enough!' whispered Zina.

'Will you protect her from hurt, Prince? Will your sword flash in the eyes of the slanderer or insolent wretch who dares to hurt my Zina?'

'Enough, Mamma, or I...'

'Why yes, flash it will…' mumbled the Prince. 'Only now do I begin to live… I want the wedding to be straight away, this very mi-nute… I… I want to send to Du-kha-no-vo straight away. I have di-a-monds there. I want to lay them at her feet…'

'What ardour! What rapture! What nobility of feelings!' exclaimed Maria Alexandrovna. 'And you, Prince, you could destroy yourself, withdrawing from society? I'll say it a thousand times! I am beside myself when I remember that infernal…'

'But what could I do, I was so a-fraid!' mumbled the Prince, whimpering and deeply moved. 'They wan-ted to put me in the mad-house… And I took fright.'

'The madhouse! Oh, the fiends! Oh, those inhuman people! Oh, the base treachery! Prince – I heard about it! But it's madness on those people's part! And why, why?!'

'I don't even know why myself!' the old man replied, feeling weak and sitting down in an armchair. 'I was at a ball, you know, and re-coun-ted some anecdote; and they didn't like it. Well, and there was a scene!'

'Surely not just because of that, Prince?'

'No. La-ter on I was play-ing cards with Prince Pyotr Dement-yich and was left without a sixth card. I had two kings and three queens… or, it would be better to say, three queens and two kings… No, one king! And then there were the queens too…'

'And because of that? Because of that! Oh, the infernal inhumanity! You're crying, Prince! But it won't happen now! I shall be beside you now, my Prince; I shan't part with Zina, and we'll see if they dare to say a word!… And you know, Prince, your marriage will even shock them. It'll put them to shame! They'll see that you're still capable… that is to say, they'll realise that such a beauty wouldn't have married a madman! You can lift your head proudly now. You'll look them straight in the face…'

'Why yes, I'll look them straight in the face,' mumbled the Prince, closing his eyes.

'He's gone completely limp,' thought Maria Alexandrovna. 'This is just a waste of words!'

'Prince, you're upset, I can see it; you simply must calm down and have a rest from this excitement,' she said, bending down to him maternally.

'Why yes, I'd like to lie down for a li-ttle,' he said.

'Yes, yes! Calm down, Prince! This excitement… Wait, I'll come with you myself… I'll put you to bed myself if necessary. Why are you looking at that portrait so, Prince? It's a portrait of my mother – an angel, not a woman! Oh, why isn't she here among us now! She was a righteous woman, Prince, a righteous woman! I can't call her anything else!'

'Righ-te-ous? *C'est joli*… I had a mother too… *princesse*… and – imagine – she was an ex-tra-or-dinarily plump wo-man… That's not what I wan-ted to say, though… I'm a li-ttle weak. *Adieu, ma charmante enfant*!… With pleasure I… today I… tomorrow… Well, it's all the same! *Au revoir, au revoir*!' At this point he tried to give a flourish with his hand, but slipped and almost fell on the threshold.

'Be careful, Prince! Lean on my arm,' cried Maria Alexandrovna.

'*Charmant*! *Charmant*!' he mumbled as he left. 'Only now do I be-gin to live…'

Zina remained alone. An inexpressible weight lay heavy on her soul. She felt disgust to the point of nausea. She was ready to despise herself. Her cheeks were burning. With clenched fists, gritted teeth and her head downcast, she stood without stirring from the spot. Tears of shame rolled from her eyes… At that moment the door opened, and Mozglyakov ran into the room.

CHAPTER IX

He had heard everything, everything!

He did indeed not walk in, but run, pale with agitation and rage. Zina looked at him in amazement.

'So that's the way you are!' he cried, panting. 'At long last I've found out who you are!'

'Who I am!' Zina repeated, looking at him as if he were a madman, and suddenly her eyes gleamed with anger.

'How dare you speak to me like that!' she exclaimed, stepping towards him.

'I heard everything!' Mozglyakov repeated solemnly, but somehow taking an involuntary step backwards.

'You heard? You were eavesdropping?' said Zina, looking at him with disdain.

'Yes, I was! Yes, I resolved upon a low trick, but on the other hand I found out that you're the most... I don't even know how to express myself to tell you... the way you come out looking now!' he replied, quailing more and more before Zina's gaze.

'And did you actually hear what you can accuse me of? What right do you have to accuse me? What right do you have to talk to me so insolently?'

'I? What right do I have? And you can ask that? You're marrying the Prince, but I don't have any right!... But you gave me your word, that's the thing!'

'When?'

'What do you mean, when?'

'But even this morning, when you were badgering me, I gave you the firm response that I couldn't say anything definite.'

'You didn't send me packing, though, you didn't refuse me completely; so you were holding me in reserve! So you were leading me on!'

Zina was irritated, and a painful sensation became apparent in her face, caused, it would have seemed, by a sharp, piercing inner pain; but she overcame her feeling.

'If I didn't send you packing,' she replied distinctly and without hurrying, although a barely discernible tremor could be heard in her voice, 'it was solely out of pity. You yourself implored me to wait a while, not to say "no" to you, but to take a closer look at you, "and then," you said, "then, when you're satisfied that I'm a noble man, perhaps you won't refuse me." Those were your own words at the very start of your pursuit. You can't deny them! You've dared to tell me now that I've led you on. But you yourself saw my aversion when I met with you today, two weeks sooner than you promised, and I didn't conceal that aversion in front of you, on the contrary, I displayed it. You yourself noticed it, because you yourself asked me whether I wasn't angry that you'd come back early. Be aware that people aren't leading someone on when they are unable and *unwilling* to conceal in front of him their aversion for him. You have dared to articulate that I have been keeping you in reserve. To that I shall reply to you that this was the way I reasoned about you: "Even if he isn't gifted with any great intelligence, he may be a kind man all the same, and for that reason it is possible to marry him." But now, having become convinced, to my good fortune, that you're a fool, and, to add to that, a malicious one, it only remains for me to wish you complete happiness and bon voyage. Farewell!'

Having said this, Zina turned away from him and set off slowly out of the room.

Guessing that all was lost, Mozglyakov began to seethe with rage.

'Ah! So I'm a fool,' he cried, 'so now I'm already a fool! All right! Farewell! But before I leave, I'll tell the whole town how you and your Mamma have bamboozled the Prince after getting him drunk! I'll tell everyone! You'll find out about Mozglyakov.'

Zina winced and almost stopped to reply, but, after a moment's thought, she only shrugged her shoulders disdainfully and slammed the door behind her.

At that instant Maria Alexandrovna appeared on the threshold. She had heard Mozglyakov's exclamation, guessed in a moment what was the matter and winced in fright. Mozglyakov hadn't yet left, Mozglyakov was beside the Prince, Mozglyakov would trumpet it through the town, while secrecy, if only for the shortest period of time, was essential! Maria Alexandrovna had her considerations. In a flash she had assessed all the circumstances, and a plan to pacify Mozglyakov had already been formed.

'What's the matter with you, *mon ami*?' she said, going towards him and reaching her hand out to him amicably.

'What do you mean: *mon ami*!' he exclaimed in a fury, 'after what you've done, and on top of that: *mon ami. Morgen früh*,[44] my dear madam! And do you think you'll deceive me again?'

'I'm sorry, I'm very sorry to see you in such a *strange* state of mind, Pavel Alexandrovich. What expressions! You're not even curbing your words in front of a lady.'

'In front of a lady! You... you're anything you like, but you're not a lady!' exclaimed Mozglyakov. I don't know precisely what he meant to express with his exclamation, but probably something very crushing.

Maria Alexandrovna looked him meekly in the face.

'Sit down!' she said sadly, indicating to him the armchair in which, a quarter of an hour before, the Prince had been reposing.

'But listen, in the end, Maria Alexandrovna!' exclaimed the perplexed Mozglyakov. 'You look at me as though you weren't at fault at all, but as though it were I at fault before you! I mean, you just can't do that!... that tone!... I mean, in the end it exceeds the limit of human patience... do you know that?'

'My friend!' Maria Alexandrovna replied, 'you'll permit me to continue to call you by that name, because you have no better friend than me; my friend! You're suffering, you're in torment, you've been wounded to the very heart – and so it's not surprising that you speak to me in such a tone. But I've resolved to reveal everything to you, the whole of my heart, particularly as I myself feel somewhat at fault before you. Do sit down, we'll have a talk.'

Maria Alexandrovna's voice was painfully soft.

Suffering was reflected in her face. The astonished Mozglyakov sat down in an armchair beside her.

'Were you eavesdropping?' she continued, looking him reproachfully in the face.

'Yes, I was! It would be a wonder if I hadn't been; I would have been a dolt then! At least I found out everything you're planning against me,' Mozglyakov replied rudely, heartening and egging himself on with his own anger.

'Even you, with your upbringing, with your principles, even you could resolve upon such a deed? Oh, good heavens!'

Mozglyakov even leapt up from his chair.

'But Maria Alexandrovna!' he exclaimed, 'it's intolerable listening to it, in the end! Remember what *you* resolved upon with *your* principles, and then condemn other people!'

'Another question,' she said, without replying to his comments, 'who gave you the idea of eavesdropping, who told you, who's been spying here? That's what I want to know.'

'Well, excuse me – that I won't say.'

'All right. I'll find out myself. I said, Paul, that I was at fault before you. But if you analyse everything, all the circumstances, then you'll see that if I am at fault, it's solely in that I wished you the greatest possible good.'

'Me? Good? That really is the limit! I can assure you that you won't fool me any more! I'm not the boy you thought!'

And he turned around in the armchair in such a way that it began creaking.

'Please, my friend, be more composed, if you can. Hear me out attentively and you'll agree with me about everything. Firstly, I intended explaining everything to you straight away, everything, and you would have learnt of the whole business from me, down to the smallest detail, without stooping to eavesdropping. And if I didn't have things out with you in advance, a little while ago, it was solely because the whole business was still in the planning. It might not have happened. You see: I'm completely candid with you. Secondly, don't reproach my daughter. She loves you to distraction, and it cost me an unbelievable effort to deflect her away from you and get her to consent to accept the Prince's proposal.'

'I had the pleasure just now of hearing the fullest proof of that love *to distraction*,' said Mozglyakov ironically.

'All right. And how did you speak to her? Should a man in love be speaking like that? Ultimately, does a man of good tone speak like that? You insulted and irritated her.'

'Well, this is no time for tone now, Maria Alexandrovna. And a little while ago, when you were both making such sweet faces at me, once I'd gone off with the Prince you started slating me! You vilified me – that's what I'm saying to you! I know everything, everything!'

'And from that same sordid source, I expect?' remarked Maria Alexandrovna, smiling disdainfully. 'Yes, Pavel Alexandrovich. I vilified you, I maligned you and, I admit, I made no little effort. But the very fact alone that I was compelled to vilify you before her, maybe even slander you – that alone proves how hard it was for me to wrest from her her agreement to abandon you! You short-sighted man! If she didn't love you, would I have had to vilify you, present you in a ridiculous, unworthy light, resort to such extreme methods? You don't yet know everything! I had to use the power of a mother to wrest you from her heart, and after an unbelievable effort I achieved only outward agreement. If you were eavesdropping on us just now, then you must have noticed that not with a single word, not with a single gesture did she support me before the Prince. During the whole scene she said hardly a word; she sang like an automaton. Her entire soul was in anguish, and, out of pity for her, in the end I took the Prince away from here. I'm certain she cried when left alone. When you came in here, you must have noticed her tears…'

Mozglyakov did, indeed, remember that when he had run into the room he had noticed Zina was in tears.

'But you, you, why were you against me, Maria Alexandrovna?' he exclaimed. 'Why did you vilify me, slander me – as you yourself now admit you did?'

'Ah, that's another matter! Now if you'd asked that sensibly at the beginning, you'd have had a reply long ago. Yes, you're right! I did it all, and I alone! Don't mix Zina up in it. Why did I do it? My reply: firstly, for Zina. The Prince is rich, distinguished, well-connected, and by marrying him, Zina will make a brilliant match. Finally, if he dies – perhaps even soon, because we're all more or less mortal – then Zina is a young widow, a princess, in high society, and perhaps very rich. Then she can marry anyone she likes, she can make the wealthiest match. But, it stands to reason, she'll marry the man she loves, the man she loved before, whose heart she tore apart by marrying the Prince. Repentance alone would compel her to make amends for her misdeed to the man she loved before.'

'Hm!' grunted Mozglyakov, looking pensively at his boots.

'Secondly – and I'll only mention this briefly,' Maria Alexandrovna continued, 'because you may not even understand it. You read your Shakespeare, deriving all your lofty feelings from him, but in reality, although you're *very good*, you're nonetheless too young – whereas I'm a mother, Pavel Alexandrovich! So listen: I'm marrying Zina to the Prince partly for the Prince himself as well, because I want to save him with this marriage. Even before, I loved that noble, that oh so kindly, that chivalrously honest old man. We were friends. He's unhappy in the claws of that infernal woman. She'll drive him to his grave. As God's my witness, I got Zina to agree to this marriage only by setting out before her all the sanctity of her feat of selflessness. She was carried away by nobility of feelings, by the charm of the feat. In her too there's something chivalrous. I presented it to her as a highly Christian thing to be the support, the consolation, the friend, the child, the beauty, the idol of a man who may have only a year left to live. Not some vile woman, not fear, not despondency would surround him in the last days of his life, but light, friendship, love. Those last days, with the sun setting, would seem to him like paradise! Where ever is the egotism in that, do tell me, please! It's more like the feat of a sister of mercy, not egotism!'

'So you… so you did it only for the Prince, as the feat of a sister of mercy?' Mozglyakov muttered in a sarcastic voice.

'I understand that question, Pavel Alexandrovich; it's quite clear. Maybe you think that the benefit to the Prince is Jesuitically interwoven here with personal benefits? Well, maybe I did indeed have those calculations in my head, only they weren't Jesuitical, but involuntary. I know you're amazed at such a candid admission, but one thing I ask of you, Pavel Alexandrovich: don't mix Zina up in this thing! She's as pure as a dove; she isn't calculating; she knows only how to love, my sweet child! If someone was calculating, then it was I, and I alone! But firstly, ask sternly of your own conscience and tell me: who, in my place, wouldn't be calculating in a case like this? We calculate the benefits to ourselves even in our most magnanimous, even in our most unselfish dealings, we calculate imperceptibly, involuntarily! Of course, almost everyone deceives themselves, assuring themselves that they're acting out of nobility alone. I don't want to deceive myself: I confess that, for all the nobility of my aims, I have been calculating. But ask if I've been calculating for myself? I don't need anything now, Pavel Alexandrovich, I've had my day. I was calculating for her, for my angel, for my child, and in that case, what sort of mother can blame me?'

Tears began shining in Maria Alexandrovna's eyes. Pavel Alexandrovich had listened in amazement to this candid confession, blinking in bewilderment.

'Well yes, what sort of mother...' he said finally. 'You sing well, Maria Alexandrovna, but... but you gave me your word, didn't you! You gave me hope too... How do you think I feel? Just think! I mean, I'm left with my nose right out of joint now, you know!'

'But do you really suppose that I haven't been thinking about you, *mon cher Paul*! On the contrary: in all these calculations there's been such enormous benefit for you, and that was the main thing that compelled me to carry out this entire enterprise.'

'Benefit to me!' exclaimed Mozglyakov, this time completely stupefied. 'How's that?'

'Good heavens! Is it really possible to be simple and short-sighted to such a degree?' Maria Alexandrovna exclaimed, raising her eyes to the heavens. 'Oh, youth, youth! This is what immersing yourself in that Shakespeare means, daydreaming, imagining we're living – living through another man's mind and another man's thoughts! You ask, my *good* Pavel Alexandrovich, where's the benefit in this for you? Permit me for the sake of clarity to make a digression: Zina loves you – there's no doubt of it! But I've noticed that, despite her evident love, there lurks within her a sort of mistrust of you, of your good feelings, of your inclinations. I've noticed that sometimes, as if on purpose, she holds herself back and she's cold with you – the fruit of much thought and mistrust. Haven't you noticed it yourself, Pavel Alexandrovich?'

'I have no-ticed; even today... However, what is it you're trying to say, Maria Alexandrovna?'

'There, you see, you've noticed it yourself. So I wasn't mistaken, then. There is within her precisely some strange sort of mistrust regarding the constancy of your good inclinations. I'm a mother – and can I fail to divine the heart of my child? Imagine now that, instead of

85

running into the room with reproaches and even oaths, instead of irritating, offending, insulting her, pure, beautiful and proud as she is, and thus unwittingly confirming her in her suspicions regarding your bad inclinations – imagine you had taken this news meekly, with tears of regret, maybe even of despair, but with lofty nobility of spirit too…'

'Hm!…'

'No, don't cut me short, Pavel Alexandrovich. I want to paint the entire picture for you, one which will strike your imagination. Imagine that you've come to her and you say: "Zinaida! I love you more than my life, but family reasons are parting us. I understand those reasons. They are for your happiness, and I no longer dare to rise up against them, Zinaida! I forgive you. Be happy, if you can!" And at that point you would have directed your gaze at her – the gaze of a sacrificial lamb, if I can put it that way – imagine all that, and think what an impact those words would have had on her heart!'

'Yes, Maria Alexandrovna, let's assume it's all so; I understand all of that… but what of it? I'd have said that, but I'd have gone away with nothing all the same…'

'No, no, no, my friend! Don't interrupt me! I want to be sure to paint the entire picture with all the consequences, to leave you nobly struck. Just imagine that you meet her later on, after some time, in high society; you meet at a ball somewhere, with brilliant lighting, with ravishing music, amidst the most magnificent women, and, in the midst of all these festivities, you, alone, sad, pensive, pale, leaning on a pillar somewhere (but in such a way that you're visible), you're watching her in the whirlwind of the ball. She's dancing. Washing around you are the ravishing sounds of Strauss,[45] the wit of high society is pouring forth, but you're alone, pale, and crushed by your passion! What will be the effect on Zinaida then, do you think? With what eyes will she look at you? "And I," she'll think, "I doubted that man who sacrificed everything, everything for me, and tore his heart asunder for me!" It stands to reason, her former love would revive inside her with irrepressible strength!'

Maria Alexandrovna stopped to draw breath. Mozglyakov turned in his armchair with such force that again it creaked. Maria Alexandrovna continued.

'For the Prince's health, Zina goes abroad, to Italy, to Spain – to Spain, where there are myrtles, lemon trees, where there's the blue sky, where there's the Guadalquivir – where there's a land of love, where it's impossible to live and not love; where roses and kisses are, so to speak, in the air! You go there too, after her; you sacrifice your work, connections, everything! There your love begins with irrepressible strength; love, youth, Spain – good heavens! It stands to reason, your love is chaste, sacred; but, finally, you *languish*, looking at one another. You understand me, *mon ami*! Of course, there will be base, treacherous people, fiends who will claim that it wasn't kindred feeling for a suffering old man that drew you abroad at all. I deliberately called your love chaste, because those people may well attach a quite different significance to it. But I'm a mother, Pavel Alexandrovich, and will I teach you anything bad?... Of course, the Prince will be in no state to supervise the two of you, but what of it? Can such a vile slander be based on that? Finally he dies, blessing his lot.

'Tell me: who will Zina marry, if not you? You're related to the Prince so distantly that there can't be any obstacles to the marriage. You take her, young, rich, distinguished – and when? – when the most distinguished of grandees might be proud to marry her! Through her you find yourself at home in the very highest social circle; through her you suddenly get a significant post, you achieve high rank. You have a hundred and fifty souls now, but then you'll be rich; the Prince will arrange everything in his will; I take that upon myself. And finally, most importantly, she is by then completely sure of you, of your heart, of your feelings, and you suddenly become for her a hero of virtue and selflessness!... And you, you ask after this where the benefit is for you? But I mean, ultimately you have to be blind not to notice, not to grasp, not to calculate that benefit, when it's standing two paces in front of you, looking at you, smiling at you, and itself saying: "It's I that am the benefit to you!" Pavel Alexandrovich, for pity's sake!'

'Maria Alexandrovna!' exclaimed Mozglyakov in extraordinary agitation, 'now I understand everything! I acted rudely, basely and ignobly!'

He leapt up from the chair and grabbed hold of his hair.

'And without calculation,' added Maria Alexandrovna, 'most importantly: without calculation!'

'I'm an ass, Maria Alexandrovna!' he exclaimed, almost in despair. 'Now everything's lost, because I love her to distraction!'

'Perhaps not everything's lost,' said Mrs Moskalyova quietly, as though thinking something over.

'Oh, if only it were possible! Help me, teach me, save me!'

And Mozglyakov burst into tears.

'My friend!' said Maria Alexandrovna sympathetically, offering him her hand, 'you did it out of excessive feverish haste, out of seething passion, and thus it was out of love for her! You were in despair, you were beside yourself! She ought to understand all that, didn't she...'

'I love her to distraction and I'm ready to sacrifice everything for her!' cried Mozglyakov.

'Listen, I'll make your excuses to her...'

'Maria Alexandrovna!'

'Yes, I take it upon myself! I'll bring you together. You'll put everything to her, everything, as I've just been putting it to you!'

'Oh God, how good you are, Maria Alexandrovna!... But... can't it be done right now?'

'God forbid! Oh, how inexperienced you are, my friend! She's so proud! She'll take it for more rudeness, for impertinence! I'll arrange everything tomorrow, but for now – go away somewhere, even go to that merchant's... come back in the evening, maybe; but I wouldn't recommend you do!'

'I'll go, I'll go! Good heavens! You're reviving me! But one more question: well, and what if the Prince doesn't die so quickly?'

'Ah good heavens, how naive you are, *mon cher Paul*! On the contrary, we must pray to God for his health. With all our heart we must wish that dear, that good, that chivalrously honest old man long life! I shall be the first to pray, tearfully, both day and night, for my daughter's happiness. But alas, it seems the Prince's health is unreliable! What's more, he'll be obliged to visit the capital now, to bring Zina out into society. I'm afraid, oh, I'm afraid it might finally finish him off! But – we shall pray, *cher Paul*, and the rest is in the hand of God!... You're going already! I give you my blessing, *mon ami*!

Have hope, be patient, take heart, most importantly – take heart! I've never doubted the nobility of your feelings…'

She shook his hand firmly, and Mozglyakov went out of the room on tiptoe.

'Well, that's one idiot I've seen off!' she said triumphantly. 'There remain the others…'

The door opened, and in came Zina. She was paler than usual. Her eyes were sparkling.

'Mamma!' she said, 'finish things quickly, or I won't be able to bear it! This is all so dirty and vile that I'm ready to run away from home. Don't go tormenting me, don't irritate me! I feel sick, do you hear: all this dirt makes me feel sick!'

'Zina! What's the matter with you, my angel? You… you were eavesdropping!' Maria Alexandrovna exclaimed, staring at Zina with disquiet.

'Yes, I was. Do you want to try and make me feel ashamed, like that idiot? Listen, I swear to you that if you torment me like this any more and give me all sorts of low roles in this low comedy, then I shall drop everything and finish with everything at once. It's quite enough that I've resolved upon the main low deed! But… I didn't know myself! I'll choke on this stench!…' And she left the room, slamming the doors.

Maria Alexandrovna stared after her and fell into thought.

'Hurry, hurry!' she exclaimed, rousing herself. 'The main difficulty, the main danger is her, and if all these scoundrels don't leave us alone, if they trumpet things around town – which *has* been done, for sure – then all's lost! She won't be able to bear all this hubbub and she'll give it up. The Prince must be taken away to the country at all costs and at once! I'll dash out there myself first, I'll extract that blockhead of mine and bring him back here. He ought to be at least of some use for something at long last! And then the other one will have had a good sleep – and we'll be off!' She rang the bell.

'What about the horses?' she asked the man who came in.

'They've long been ready, ma'am,' the servant replied.

The horses had been ordered just as Maria Alexandrovna had been taking the Prince upstairs.

She put on her things, but first popped into Zina's room to inform her, in broad terms, of her decision, and to give certain instructions. But Zina couldn't listen to her. She was lying in bed with her face in the pillows; she was in floods of tears and with her white arms bared to the elbows, she was tearing at her wonderful long hair. Occasionally she would shudder, as though the cold were passing in an instant through all of her limbs. Maria Alexandrovna tried starting to speak, but Zina didn't even raise her head.

After standing over her for some time, Maria Alexandrovna left the room in confusion, and to compensate herself with something else, she got into the carriage and ordered the horses to be driven at top speed.

'It's not good that Zina was eavesdropping!' she thought, sitting in the carriage. 'I persuaded Mozglyakov with almost the same words as I did her. She's proud, and maybe she was insulted... Hm! But the most important thing, the most important thing is to manage to arrange everything before they've got wind of it! Calamity! Well, and as ill luck would have it, my idiot husband's not at home!...'

And at this thought alone, a fury took hold of her which did not bode well for Afanasy Matveyich; she twisted and turned in her seat in impatience. The horses sped her along at full pelt.

CHAPTER X

The carriage was flying. We've already said that as early as that morning, when she was chasing around the town after the Prince, a brilliant idea flashed through Maria Alexandrovna's mind. We promised to mention the idea in the appropriate place. But the reader already knows it. The idea was for her in her turn to confiscate the Prince and take him away as quickly as possible to the village outside of town where the blissful Afanasy Matveyich was serenely flourishing.

We shan't conceal that a kind of inexplicable disquiet was descending upon Maria Alexandrovna more and more. This sometimes happens even to true heroes, at precisely the time they are achieving their goal. An instinct of sorts was telling her it was dangerous to remain in Mordasov. 'And then once we're in the country,' she reasoned, 'the whole town can turn itself upside down!' Of course, there was no time to lose in the country either. Anything might happen, anything, absolutely anything, although, of course, we don't believe the rumours spread subsequently about my heroine by plotters that at this moment she was even afraid of the police. In short, she could see that Zina and the Prince had to be married as quickly as possible. The means were near to hand. The village priest could marry them at the house. They could be married even the day after next; in the absolutely last resort, even the next day. After all, there were weddings arranged in two hours! This haste, this absence of any kind of festivities, betrothals, parties for the bride, could be presented to the Prince as essential *comme il faut*; it could be suggested to him that this was more seemly, grander. Finally, it could all be presented as a romantic adventure, and thus the most sensitive string in the Prince's heart could be touched. In the last resort, he could even be given too much to drink, or, even better, kept continually drunk. And then, whatever might happen, Zina would be a princess anyway! If a scandal was unavoidable later on, in St Petersburg or Moscow, for example, where the Prince had relatives, one had one's consolation even so. Firstly, this was all still in the future, and secondly, Maria Alexandrovna believed that scandal was hardly ever avoidable in high society, especially in matrimonial affairs; that it was even good form, although high society scandals, in her understanding,

91

ought always to be somehow special, grandiose, something in the manner of *Monte Cristo* or *Mémoires du Diable*.[46] And finally, Zina would only have to appear in high society, and her Mamma to support her, for everyone, absolutely everyone to be conquered at that very instant, and not one of all those countesses and princesses would be in any condition to withstand the Mordasovan dressing-down that only Maria Alexandrovna was capable of giving them, all at once or individually.

It was as a result of all these considerations that Maria Alexandrovna was now flying to her estate to fetch Afanasy Matveyich, for whom, according to her calculations, there was now an imminent essential need. Indeed: taking the Prince to the country meant taking him to Afanasy Matveyich, with whom the Prince might not want to become acquainted. But if Afanasy Matveyich himself issued an invitation, then the matter took on a completely different complexion. What's more, the appearance of an elderly and imposing paterfamilias, coming specially from distant parts at the first word of the Prince in white tie and tails and with hat in hand, might have an extremely pleasant effect, might even flatter the Prince's self-esteem. And such an insistent and formal invitation is hard to refuse, thought Maria Alexandrovna. Finally the carriage had flown the three versts, and Sofron the coachman reined his horses in by the porch of a long, single-storied, wooden building, quite ancient and blackened by time, with a long row of windows and surrounded on all sides by old lime trees. This was Maria Alexandrovna's country house and summer residence. Lights were already burning in the house.

'Where is the blockhead?' cried Maria Alexandrovna, bursting into a room like a hurricane. 'What's this towel doing here? Ah, he's been drying himself! Has he been in the bath-house again? And forever swilling down his tea! Well, what are you goggling at me for, you arrant fool? Why hasn't his hair been trimmed? Grishka! Grishka! Grishka! Why haven't you given the master a haircut as I ordered last week?'

When entering the room, Maria Alexandrovna had been intending to greet Afanasy Matveyich much more gently, but on seeing that he had come from the bath-house and was enjoying himself drinking tea, she couldn't refrain from the bitterest indignation. Indeed: so much effort and trouble on her part, and so much utterly blissful quietism on the part of Afanasy Matveyich, a man totally superfluous and incapable of doing anything; such a contrast stung her right to the heart at once. Meanwhile, the blockhead, or, to put it more courteously, the one who was called the blockhead, sat by the samovar and gazed, with his mouth open and eyes goggling, in foolish fright at his spouse, whose appearance had all but petrified him. In from the entrance hall leant the sleepy, clumsy figure of Grishka, who stared blankly at this entire scene.

'He doesn't let me, that's why I haven't cut it,' he said in a grumpy, hoarse voice. 'Ten times I've come up with the scissors – the mistress, I says, 'll soon be here – both of us'll catch it, and what'll we do then? No, he says, wait, I'm putting my hair in waves for Sunday; I need to have my hair long.'

'What? So he puts his hair in waves! So you've come up with the idea of putting your hair in waves when I'm not here? What kind of fashions are these? And does it suit you, does it suit your silly head? God, what a mess we have here! What's that smell? I'm asking you, you fiend, what's that smell here?' the wife cried, falling more and more upon the innocent, and by now utterly crazed Afanasy Matveyich.

'Mo-Mother!' mumbled the cowed spouse without rising from his seat, and looking at the mistress with pleading eyes, 'Mo-Mo-Mother!…'

'How many times have I tried beating it into your ass's head that I'm not in the least your mother? How can I be your mother, pygmy that you are! How dare you give such a name to a noble lady whose place is in high society and not beside such an ass as you!'

'But… but you are, Maria Alexandrovna, my lawful wife, after all, and so I say… in a conjugal way…' Afanasy Matveyich began to object, at the same time raising both his arms to his head to shield his hair.

'Oh, you son of a bitch! Oh, you loggerhead! Why, has anything more stupid ever been heard than a reply like that? Lawful wife! What lawful wives are there nowadays? Would anyone at all in high society nowadays use that stupid, that seminarial, that disgustingly low word "*lawful*"? And how dare you remind me that I'm your wife, when I'm trying with all my might, with all the power of my soul to forget about it?

Why are you covering your head with your arms? Look, what state is his hair in? Soaking, soaking wet! It won't dry in three hours! How can I take him now? How can I show him to people now? What am I to do now?'

And Maria Alexandrovna wrung her hands in fury, running to and fro across the room. The problem was, of course, not a major one, and it was corrigible; but the fact is that Maria Alexandrovna couldn't control her all-conquering and power-loving spirit. She felt the need for an incessant outpouring of her anger onto Afanasy Matveyich, because tyranny is a habit which turns into a need. Well, and in the end, everyone knows what a contrast some refined ladies of a certain society are capable of at home behind the scenes, and I specifically wanted to depict that contrast. Afanasy Matveyich followed his spouse's manoeuvres with trepidation, and even broke out in a sweat just looking at her.

'Grishka!' she finally exclaimed, 'the master needs to dress right away! Tailcoat, trousers, white tie, waistcoat – look lively! And where's his hairbrush, where's the brush?'

'Mother! But I've come from the bath-house, you know: I may catch cold, if I travel to town…'

'You won't catch cold!'

'But my hair's wet and…'

'Well, and now we're going to dry it! Grishka, bring the hairbrush, rub him dry, harder! Harder! That's it! That's it!'

At this command the zealous and devoted Grishka began rubbing his master's hair as hard as he could, seizing him by the shoulder and bending a little towards the couch for greater convenience. Afanasy Matveyich, almost crying, winced.

'Now come here! Lift him up, Grishka! Where's the pomade? Bend down, bend down, you good-for-nothing – bend down, you sponger!'

And Maria Alexandrovna personally set about pomading her spouse, pulling pitilessly at his thick, greying hair, which, to his cost, he hadn't had cut. Afanasy Matveyich grunted and sighed, yet didn't cry out, and bore the entire operation submissively.

'You've sucked the juices out of me, sloven that you are!' said Maria Alexandrovna. 'Bend down even further, bend down!'

'And how, Mother, have I sucked the juices out of you?' mumbled her spouse, bending his head down as far as he possibly could.

'Blockhead! He doesn't understand allegories! Now comb your hair; and you get him dressed, and look lively!'

Our heroine settled down in an armchair and inquisitorially supervised the entire ritual of Afanasy Matveyich's robing. Meanwhile, he had time to have something of a rest and pull himself together, and when it came to the tying of the white tie, he even dared to express some opinion of his own regarding the form and beauty of the knot. Finally, when putting on his tails, the venerable husband cheered up completely and began throwing glances at himself in the mirror with a certain respect.

'Where is it you're taking me, Maria Alexandrovna?' he said, preening himself.

Maria Alexandrovna could hardly believe her ears.

'Do you hear that? Oh, you scarecrow! How dare you ask me where I'm taking you!'

'Mother, I mean, I do need to know…'

'Silence! Just you call me Mother one more time, especially where we're going now! You'll sit for a whole month without tea!'

The frightened spouse fell silent.

'Look! You haven't earned a single cross, have you, ragamuffin that you are,' she continued, looking scornfully at Afanasy Matveyich's black tailcoat.

Afanasy Matveyich finally took offence.

'Crosses, Mother, are given by the authorities; and I'm a Councillor, not a ragamuffin,' he said in noble indignation.

'What, what, what? So you've learnt to argue here! Oh, you peasant you! Oh you snivelling wretch! Well, it's a pity I haven't got the time to deal with you now, or else I'd… Well, but I'll remember later on! Give him his hat, Grishka! Give him his fur coat! Tidy up all three of these rooms here while I'm gone; and tidy up the green, corner room too. Brushes in hands instantly! Take the covers off the mirrors, off the clocks too, and I want everything ready in an hour. And you put on a tailcoat too, and hand gloves out to the servants, do you hear, Grishka, do you hear?'

They got into the carriage. Afanasy Matveyich was perplexed and surprised. Maria Alexandrovna, meanwhile, was wondering to herself how she could knock certain instructions, essential to him in his present position, most comprehensibly into her spouse's head. But her spouse forestalled her.

'I had a most original dream today, Maria Alexandrovna,' he announced, quite unexpectedly, in the midst of their shared silence.

'Confound you, you damned scarecrow! I was thinking, and then God knows what! Some dream or other! How dare you bother me with your peasant's dreams! Original! Do you even understand what original means? Listen, I'm telling you for the last time, if you dare to mention just one word today about a dream or about anything else, then I – I really don't know what I'll do to you! Listen carefully: Prince K. has come to visit me. Do you remember Prince K.?'

'I do, Mother, I do. And why is it he's come to see you?'

'Be quiet, it's none of your business! With especial courtesy, as the master of the house, you must ask him to our village straight away. That's why I'm taking you. We're going to get into the carriage and set off this very day. But if you just dare to say so much as one word the whole evening, or tomorrow, or the day after tomorrow, or ever, I'll have you tending the geese for a whole year. Don't say anything, not a single word. That's your entire responsibility, do you understand?'

'Well, and if I'm asked something?'

'Keep quiet all the same.'

'But, I mean, I can't keep quiet all the time, Maria Alexandrovna.'

'In that case answer in monosyllables, something such as, for example, "hm!", or something of the sort, to show that you're an intelligent man and that you think things over before answering.'

'Hm.'

'Understand what I'm doing! I'm taking you so that, having heard about the Prince, and in raptures at his visit, you've come flying to see him at once to show your esteem and ask him to your village; do you understand?'

'Hm.'

'You don't go "hm" now, you fool! You answer me.'

'Very well, Mother, everything will be as you say; only why am I going to invite the Prince?'

'What, what? Arguing again! What's it got to do with you: why? How dare you ask about that?'

'What I'm driving at, Maria Alexandrovna, is how am I going to invite him, if you've ordered me to keep quiet?'

'I'll do the talking for you, and you just bow, do you hear, just bow, and hold your hat in your hands. Do you understand?'

'I understand, Mo... Maria Alexandrovna.'

'The Prince is extremely witty. If he says anything, even if not to you, then you reply to everything with a genial and cheerful smile, do you hear?'

'Hm.'

'Again you've started going "hm"! Don't go "hm" with me! Give me a straight and simple answer: do you hear or not?'

'I hear, Maria Alexandrovna, I hear, how can I fail to hear, and I'm going "hm" to get myself used to saying it, as you ordered. Only my point's still the same, Mother. How's it to be: if the Prince says something, then you order me to gaze at him and smile. Well, but all the same, if I'm asked something?'

'What a slow-witted dolt! I've already told you: keep quiet. I'll answer for you, and you just look and smile.'

'But, I mean, he'll think I'm dumb,' said Afanasy Matveyich.

'What does that matter? Let him think it; at least you'll conceal the fact that you're a fool.'

'Hm... Well, and if other people ask about anything?'

'Nobody will ask anything, there won't be anyone there. But if, just in case – which God forbid! – if anyone does come, and if they ask you anything or say anything, then reply at once with a sarcastic smile. Do you know what a sarcastic smile is?'

'It's a witty one, is it, Mother?'

'I'll give you a witty one, blockhead! Who's going to ask for wit from you, you fool? A mocking smile, do you understand – mocking and disdainful.'

'Hm.'

'Oh, I'm worried about this blockhead!' Maria Alexandrovna whispered to herself. 'He's sworn to suck all the juices out of me for sure! It really would have been better not to bring him at all!'

As she pondered thus, anxious and lamenting, Maria Alexandrovna was incessantly looking out of the window of her conveyance and urging the coachman on. The horses were flying, yet all the time it seemed to her but slowly. Afanasy Matveyich sat silently in his corner, going over his lessons in his head. Finally the carriage drove into town and stopped at Maria Alexandrovna's house. But no sooner had our heroine managed to jump out onto the porch than she suddenly saw a two-horse, two-seat sleigh with a hood approaching the house, the one in which Anna Nikolayevna Antipova usually drove out. In the sleigh sat two ladies. One of them, it stands to reason, was Anna Nikolayevna herself, and the other was Natalya Dmitriyevna, in recent times her sincere friend and acolyte. Maria Alexandrovna's heart sank. But she hadn't had time to cry out before another conveyance drove up, a closed sleigh, confined inside which there was evidently some other guest. Joyous exclamations rang out:

'Maria Alexandrovna! And with Afanasy Matveyich! You're here! Where have you been? How opportune, since we're coming to you for the whole evening! What a surprise!'

The guests jumped out onto the porch and started twittering like swallows. Maria Alexandrovna couldn't believe her eyes and ears.

'Damn you!' she thought to herself. 'This smells like a conspiracy! It needs to be investigated! But… you magpies won't outwit me!… You wait!…'

CHAPTER XI

Mozglyakov left Maria Alexandrovna apparently quite comforted. She had fired him up completely. He didn't go to Boroduyev's, as he felt the need for seclusion. An extraordinary influx of heroic and romantic dreams was giving him no peace. He dreamt of a solemn discussion with Zina, then of the noble tears of his all-forgiving heart, pallor and despair at a brilliant St Petersburg ball, Spain, the Guadalquivir, love, and the dying Prince joining their hands just before his final hour. Then of his beautiful wife, devoted to him and constantly wondering at his heroism and lofty feelings; of the attention, passing and surreptitious, of some countess from the 'high society' in which he was sure to find himself through his marriage to Zina, Prince K.'s widow; of a post as a vice-governor, money – in short, everything so eloquently painted by Maria Alexandrovna passed once more through his utterly contented soul, caressing and enticing it, and, most importantly, flattering his self-esteem.

But then – and I truly don't know how to explain it – when he had already begun to feel tired out by all these raptures, a very annoying thought suddenly occurred to him: that this was all, in any event, still in the future, wasn't it, whereas now he was, all the same, left with his nose well out of joint.

When this thought occurred to him, he noticed that he had wandered to somewhere a long way off, to some secluded suburb of Mordasov that was unfamiliar to him. It was getting dark. Along streets lined by tiny little houses sunk into the ground there was the fierce barking of the dogs which breed in horrifying numbers in provincial towns, and in precisely those districts where there's nothing to guard and nothing to steal. Wet snow was beginning to fall. He would occasionally encounter some petty bourgeois out late or a peasant woman in a sheepskin coat and boots. For some unknown reason, all this started to make Pavel Alexandrovich angry – a very bad sign, because given a good turn of events, everything appears to us, on the contrary, nice and cheerful. Pavel Alexandrovich involuntarily remembered that up until now he had constantly set the tone in Mordasov; he had very much enjoyed being given hints in every house that he was a bridegroom-to-be, and being congratulated on this virtue. He was even proud of being a bridegroom-to-be. And now suddenly he would appear in front of everyone – in retirement! And there'd be laughter. After all, he really couldn't go disabusing them all, telling them about the balls with the columns in St Petersburg and about the Guadalquivir. Pondering, miserable and lamenting, he finally hit upon an idea which had already been scratching imperceptibly at his heart for some time: 'Was it all true? Would it all turn out the way Maria Alexandrovna had painted it?' At this point he remembered, incidentally, that Maria Alexandrovna was an extremely cunning lady, that, however worthy of universal respect, she was nonetheless a gossip and lied from dawn till dusk. That having now removed him, she'd probably had her own special reasons for doing so, and that ultimately anyone can be good at painting. He thought about Zina too; he remembered her farewell look, which had been far from expressing a secret passionate love; and at the same time remembered, incidentally, that he had, after all, an hour before, swallowed her calling him a fool. At the memory of this, Pavel Alexandrovich suddenly stopped, as though rooted to the ground, and blushed to the point of tears with shame.

As luck would have it, the next minute something unpleasant happened to him: he stumbled, and flew off the wooden footpath into a snowdrift. While he was floundering in the snow, the pack of dogs which had already long been pursuing him with its barking flew at him from all sides. One of them, the smallest and most fervid, even stayed hanging on to him, having taken hold of the flap of his fur coat with its teeth. Beating the dogs off, swearing out loud and even cursing his fate, Pavel Alexandrovich, with a ripped coat flap and unbearable misery in his soul, finally made his way to the end of the street, and only then noticed that he was lost. It's well known that someone who is lost in an unfamiliar part of town, especially at night, cannot possibly walk straight down the street; some unknown force continually urges him to be sure to turn off into every street and side-street he encounters on his way. Following this system, Pavel Alexandrovich got completely lost. 'To hell with all these lofty ideas!' he said to himself, spitting with anger. 'And may the Devil himself take you all with your lofty feelings and your Guadalquivirs!' I can't say Mozglyakov was attractive at that moment.

Finally, tired, worn out after wandering lost for two hours, he reached the porch of Maria Alexandrovna's house. Seeing a number of conveyances, he was surprised. 'Surely not guests, surely not a guest-night?' he thought. 'But to what end?' Having enquired of a servant he encountered and learnt that Maria Alexandrovna had been in the country and had brought Afanasy Matveyich back with her wearing a white tie, and that the Prince had already woken up, but not yet come down to the guests, without so much as a word, Pavel Alexandrovich went upstairs to see his uncle. At that moment he was in precisely that frame of mind when a man of weak character is able, spurred on by revenge, to resolve upon some dreadful, really malicious trick, without thinking of how he might have to repent of it for the rest of his life.

Going upstairs, he found the Prince asleep in an armchair in front of his travelling toilette, completely bare-headed, but already wearing his imperial and side-whiskers. His wig was in the hands of his grey-haired, ancient valet and favourite, Ivan Pakhomych. Pakhomych was combing it, thoughtfully and deferentially. And as regards the Prince, he was a very sorry sight, not having yet come round after his recent drinking bout. He sat all saggy somehow, looking blank, haggard and limp, and gazing at Mozglyakov as though he didn't recognise him.

'How's your health, Uncle?' asked Mozglyakov.

'What... is it you?' his uncle said finally. 'I fell asleep for a bit, brother. Oh good heavens!' he cried, becoming all animated, 'I'm... without my wig, aren't I!'

'Don't worry, Uncle! I... I'll help you, if you like.'

'But you've gone and found out my secret now! I said the door should be locked, didn't I? Well, my friend, you must give me your word of ho-nour im-me-diately that you won't exploit my secret and won't tell anyone my hair is false.'

'Oh, for pity's sake, Uncle! Do you really consider me capable of such meanness?' exclaimed Mozglyakov, wanting to oblige the old man for... future purposes.

'Why yes, why yes! And since I can see you're a noble man, then so be it, I'll sur-prise you... and reveal all my se-crets to you. How, my dear, do you like my mou-stache?'

'It's splendid, Uncle! Amazing! How have you managed to keep it so long?'

'Be disabused, my friend, it's false!' said the Prince, looking at Pavel Alexandrovich in triumph.

'Really? It's hard to believe. Well, and the side-whiskers? Admit it, Uncle, you dye them black, don't you?'

'Dye them? Not only do I not dye them, they too are completely artificial!'

'Artificial? No, Uncle, say what you will, I don't believe it. You're making fun of me!'

'*Parole d'honneur, mon ami!*'[47] exclaimed the triumphant Prince. 'And ima-gine, everyone, ab-solutely everyone is de-ceived, just the same as you! Even Stepanida Matveyevna doesn't believe it, even though she herself sometimes sticks them on. But I'm certain, my friend, that you'll keep my secret. Give me your word of honour…'

'My word of honour, Uncle, I will. I repeat: do you really consider me capable of such meanness?'

'Ah, my friend, what a fall I had without you today! Feofil tipped me out of the carriage again.'

'Tipped you out again? But when?'

'We were already approaching the mo-na-stery…'

'I know, Uncle, a good while ago.'

'No, no, two hours ago, no more. I set off for the hermitage, and he went and tipped me out; he frigh-tened me so – my heart's in my mouth even now.'

'But Uncle, you've been asleep, haven't you!' said Mozglyakov in astonishment.

'Why yes, I have… but then I set off, although I… although maybe I… ah, how strange that is!'

'I can assure you, Uncle, you dreamt it! You've been very quietly asleep ever since after lunch.'

'Really?' And the Prince became pensive. 'Why yes, perhaps I did indeed dream it. But I remember everything I dreamt. First I dreamt of some very strange bull with horns; and then I dreamt of some pro-se-cutor, who also seemed to have horns…'

'That must be Nikolai Vasilyevich Antipov, Uncle.'

'Why yes, perhaps it's him. And then I dreamt of Napoleon Bo-naparte. You know, my friend, people keep on telling me I look like Napoleon Bo-naparte… but in profile I'm apparently strikingly like one of the old popes. What's your view, my dear, do I look like a pope?'

'I think you're more like Napoleon, Uncle.'

'Why yes, that's *en face*.[48] But I think the same myself, my dear. And I dreamt of him when he was already imprisoned on the island,[49] and, do you know, what a talkative, bright, convivial fellow he is, so he amused me im-mense-ly.'

'Is that Napoleon you're talking about, Uncle?' said Pavel Alexandrovich, looking pensively at his uncle. A strange kind of idea was beginning to flicker in his mind – an idea which he could not himself yet comprehend.

'Why yes, Na-po-leon. He and I were arguing about philosophy all the time. And you know, my friend, I'm even sorry that the… Eng-lish treated him so severely. Of course, if he hadn't been kept on a chain, he'd have started attacking people again. He was a rabid man! But it's a pity, all the same. I wouldn't have done that. I'd have put him on an un-in-ha-bited island…'

'But why an uninhabited one?' asked Mozglyakov absentmindedly.

'Well, perhaps on an in-ha-bited one, but with sensible inhabitants to be sure. Well, and with various enter-tain-ments arranged for him: theatre, music, ballet – and all paid for by the state. I'd have let him out for a walk, under supervision, it stands to reason, or else he'd have slipped away at once. He was very fond of pies of some sort. Well, and with pies made for him every day. I'd have, so to speak, supported him pa-ter-nally. And I'd have had him re-pen-ting…'

Mozglyakov listened absentmindedly to the chattering of the old man, who was only half-awake, and bit his nails in impatience. He wanted to turn the conversation to marriage – he didn't himself yet know to what end, but boundless spite was seething in his heart. Suddenly the old man cried out in surprise.

'Oh, *mon ami*! I forgot to tell you, didn't I. Imagine, I pro-posed today, you know.'

'Proposed, Uncle?' exclaimed Mozglyakov, becoming animated.

'Why yes, pro-posed. Pakhomych, are you going? Well, all right. *C'est une charmante personne...*[50] But... I confess to you, my dear, I acted preci-pit-ately. Only now do I see it. Oh, good heavens!'

'But permit me, Uncle, when ever did you propose?'

'I confess to you, my friend, I don't even know for sure when. Did I dream that too? Ah, but how strange it is!'

Mozglyakov gave a start of delight. A new idea had flashed through his mind.

'But to whom and when did you propose, Uncle?' he repeated impatiently.

'To my hostess's daughter, *mon ami... cette belle personne...*[51] but I've forgotten what her name is. Only, you see, *mon ami*, it's quite im-po-ssible for me to get married. What ever am I to do now?'

'Yes, of course, you'll destroy yourself if you get married. But permit me to ask you one more question, Uncle. Are you absolutely sure that you really did propose?'

'Why yes... I'm sure.'

'And what if you dreamt it all, in the same way as you dreamt that you'd fallen out of the carriage a second time?'

'Oh, good heavens! Indeed, perhaps I dreamt this too! And so I simply don't know how to show my face down there now. How, my friend, could I find out for cer-tain, in some in-di-rect way, whether I proposed or not? Or else, imagine, what's my position like now?'

'Do you know what, Uncle? I don't think there's even anything to find out.'

'How's that?'

'I think you dreamt it for certain.'

'I think the same myself, my dear, particularly as I often have si-mi-lar dreams.'

'There, you see, Uncle. And imagine, you had a little to drink at breakfast, then at lunch, and finally...'

'Why yes, my friend; maybe that's precisely the rea-son.'

'Particularly, Uncle, as, no matter how flushed you might have been, there's no way, all the same, you could have made such a foolhardy proposal when awake. As long as I've known you, Uncle, you've been a man sensible in the highest degree, and...'

'Why yes, why yes.'

'Imagine just one thing: if your relatives, who are ill-disposed towards you as it is, found out about this – what would happen then?'

'Oh, good heavens!' cried the frightened Prince. 'And what *would* happen then?'

'For pity's sake! They'd all cry out with one accord that you'd done this when not in your right mind, that you were mad, that you needed to be taken charge of, that you'd been deceived, and, quite likely, they'd put you away under supervision somewhere.'

Mozglyakov knew what would frighten the old man.

'Oh, good heavens!' exclaimed the Prince, shaking like a leaf. 'Would they really put me away?'

'And for that reason, you consider it, Uncle: could you have made such a foolhardy proposal when awake? You understand for yourself what's good for you. I solemnly assert that you dreamt it all.'

'I definitely did, I de-fi-nitely did!' repeated the frightened Prince. 'Ah, how cleverly you've resolved it all, my dear! I'm sincerely grateful to you for making me understand.'

'And I'm terribly glad, Uncle, that I met with you today. Imagine: without me you might really have got confused and thought you were someone's fiancé, and gone down there as a fiancé. Imagine how dangerous!'

'Why yes... yes, dangerous!'

'Just remember, that girl is twenty-three years old; nobody wants to marry her, and suddenly you, rich, distinguished, present yourself as her fiancé! They'll seize on the idea straight away, assure you that you are indeed her fiancé, and quite likely make you get married by force. And then they'll be reckoning that you may die soon.'

'Surely not!'

'And finally, remember, Uncle: a man with your merits...'

'Why yes, with my merits...'

'With your intelligence, with your courtesy...'

'Why yes, with my intelligence, yes!...'

'And you are, ultimately, a prince. Is that the sort of match you could make for yourself if for some reason you really did need to marry? Just think, what will your relatives say?'

'Ah, my friend, they'll nag me to death, you know! I've already experienced so much treachery and malice from them... Imagine, I suspect they wanted to put me in the m-ad-house. Well, forgive me, my friend, does that make any sense? Why, what would I do there... in the m-ad-house?'

'It stands to reason, Uncle, and that's why I won't leave your side when you go downstairs. There are guests there now.'

'Guests? Oh, good heavens!'

'Don't worry, Uncle, I'll be with you.'

'But how grate-ful I am to you, my dear, you're simply my saviour! But you know what? I'd better leave.'

'Tomorrow, Uncle, tomorrow, in the morning, at seven o'clock. And today, you say your goodbyes in front of everyone and say that you're leaving.'

'I shall definitely leave... for Father Misail's... But my friend, well, what if they try to arrange the ma-rriage down there?'

'Don't be afraid, Uncle, I'll be with you. And in the end, whatever's said to you, whatever's hinted at to you, say straight out that you dreamt it all... as was truly the case.'

'Why yes, I de-fi-nitely dreamt it! Only you know, my friend, it was a very char-ming dream all the same! She's astonishingly good-looking and, you know, such forms...'

'Well, goodbye, Uncle, I'll go downstairs, and you...'

'What? So you're leaving me by myself!' the Prince exclaimed in fright.

'No, Uncle, only we'll go down separately, first me, and then you. That'll be best.'

'Well, all right. Incidentally, I need to make a note of an idea.'

'Precisely, Uncle, you make a note of your idea, and then come, don't delay. Tomorrow morning...'

'And tomorrow morning to the holy father's, de-fi-nitely to the ho-ly fa-ther's! *Charmant, charmant*! But do you know, my friend, she's as-to-nishingly good-looking... such forms... and if I really did definitely need to get married, then I...'

106

'God preserve you, Uncle!'

'Why yes, God preserve me!… Well, goodbye, my dear, in a minute I'll… just make the note. *A propos*, I've wanted to ask you for a long time: have you read Casanova's memoirs?'[52]

'I have, Uncle, what of it?'

'Why yes… I've gone and for-gotten now what I wanted to say…'

'You'll remember later on, Uncle – goodbye!'

'Goodbye, my friend, goodbye! Only it was an enchanting dream, all the same, an en-chan-ting dream!…'

'We're coming to see you, all of us, all of us! Praskovya Ilyinishna's coming, and Louisa Karlovna was meaning to be here,' twittered Anna Nikolayevna, entering the salon and looking around greedily. She was quite a pretty little lady, garishly, but richly dressed and, on top of that, very well aware that she was pretty. She really did think that the Prince was hidden somewhere in a corner along with Zina.

'Katerina Petrovna's coming, ma'am, and Felisata Mikhailovna was meaning to be here too,' added Natalya Dmitriyevna, a lady of colossal size, whose forms had been so to the Prince's liking and who looked extremely like a grenadier. She was wearing an extraordinarily small pink hat, which stuck out on the back of her head. For three weeks now she had been the sincerest friend of Anna Nikolayevna, to whom she had been making up, for a long time before, trying to get round her, and whom, judging by appearances, she could have swallowed in a single gulp along with the pips.

'I won't even mention the, you might say, delight I feel, seeing you both in my house, and in the evening too,' Maria Alexandrovna began crooning, having recovered from her initial astonishment, 'but please do tell me, what miracle has urged you to come and see me today, when I'd already quite despaired of having such an honour?'

'Oh, good heavens, Maria Alexandrovna, you are a one, ma'am, truly!' said Natalya Dmitriyevna with false modesty, sweetly, bashfully and squeakily, which made for a most curious contrast with her appearance.

'*Mais, ma charmante*,'[53] Anna Nikolayevna twittered, 'you know, sometime we really must, we must without fail finish all our preparations for this theatre. Just today Pyotr Mikhailovich told Kallist Stanislavich that he's extremely distressed that we're not getting on with things very well and that all we do is quarrel. And so the four of us met today and thought: let's go to Maria Alexandrovna's and decide everything all in one go! Natalya Dmitriyevna let the others know too. Everyone's coming. So we'll reach an agreement, and it will be fine. And don't let people say that all we do is quarrel, isn't that right, *mon ange*?' she added playfully, kissing Maria Alexandrovna. 'Oh, good

heavens! Zinaida Afanasyevna! But you keep getting prettier every day!'
Anna Nikolayevna rushed to give Zina a kiss.

'Well, she has nothing else to do other than grow prettier, ma'am,'
Natalya Dmitriyevna added sweetly, rubbing her huge hands.

'Ah, the Devil take them! I didn't even think of the theatre! The
magpies have done this cleverly!' whispered Maria Alexandrovna,
beside herself with rage.

'All the more, my angel,' Anna Nikolayevna added, 'as you have the
dear Prince with you now. I mean, you know the former landowners
at Dukhanovo had a theatre. We've already made enquiries and know
that all the old scenery, the curtain and even the costumes are stored
there somewhere. The Prince was at my house today, and I was so
surprised by his arrival that I completely forgot to tell him. Now we'll
start talking about the theatre deliberately, you'll help us, and the Prince
will order all that old junk to be sent off to us. Or else who will you get
to make anything like scenery here? And the main thing is, we want to
entice the Prince into our theatre too. He definitely ought to subscribe:
it's for the poor, after all. Perhaps he'll even take a role – he's just so nice
and agreeable. Then things will go wonderfully well.'

'Of course he'll take a role. ma'am, I mean, he can be made to play
any kind of role,' added Natalya Dmitriyevna meaningfully.

Anna Nikolayevna hadn't been deceiving Maria Alexandrovna: with
every minute, ladies kept arriving. Maria Alexandrovna scarcely had
time to greet them and emit the exclamations demanded in such
instances by decorum and seemliness.

I don't undertake to describe all of the visitors. I'll say only that each
of them had an extraordinarily treacherous look. Written on all of their
faces were expectation and a sort of wild impatience. Some of the ladies
had come with the resolute intention of witnessing some extraordinary
scandal, and would be very angry if they were obliged to depart without
having seen one. Outwardly everyone behaved with extraordinary
courtesy, but Maria Alexandrovna steadfastly prepared herself for
attack. Questions about the Prince, seemingly the most natural ones,
rained down; but contained in each of them was some sort of hint or
insinuation. Tea appeared; everyone took their seats. One group took
control of the grand piano. To an invitation to play and sing, Zina

replied dryly that she wasn't so well. The pallor of her face proved it. Concerned questions immediately rained down, and even here the opportunity was found to ask and hint about a certain matter. People asked about Mozglyakov too, and they turned with these questions to Zina. Maria Alexandrovna was multiplied tenfold at this time: she saw everything that was happening in each corner of the room, heard what was being said by each of the visitors, although there were as many as ten of them, and immediately responded to all the questions, never, it stands to reason, at a loss for words. She trembled for Zina and wondered at the fact that she didn't leave, as she always had done until now in the face of similar gatherings. Afanasy Matveyich was noticed too. Everybody always made fun of him, so as to taunt Maria Alexandrovna with her spouse. But now something might be found out as well from dull-witted and candid Afanasy Matveyich. Maria Alexandrovna looked closely and with disquiet at the state of siege in which she saw her spouse. And, moreover, he replied 'hm' to every question with such an unhappy and unnatural air that there was good reason for her to fly into a fury.

'Maria Alexandrovna! Afanasy Matveyich doesn't want to talk to us at all,' exclaimed one bold, bright-eyed little lady, who was afraid of absolutely no one and never got embarrassed. 'Tell him to be a little more civil with the ladies.'

'Truly, I don't know myself what's wrong with him today,' Maria Alexandrovna replied, interrupting her conversation with Anna Nikolayevna and Natalya Dmitriyevna and smiling cheerfully, 'he is, indeed, so taciturn! Even with me he's hardly said a word. Why on earth don't you answer Felisata Mikhailovna, *Athanase*? What were you asking him?'

'But… but… Mother, I mean, you yourself…' the astonished and confused Afanasy Matveyich began mumbling. At this time he was standing by the lighted fire with his hand tucked into his waistcoat in a picturesque posture he had chosen for himself, sipping his tea. The ladies' questions had so embarrassed him that he was blushing like some slip of a girl. And when he began his justification, he met with such a terrible look from his enraged spouse that he almost fainted in fright. Not knowing what to do, wanting somehow to recover and once more earn some respect, he made to gulp down some tea; but the tea was too hot. He took an inappropriately big mouthful, scalded himself dreadfully, dropped his cup, choked, and had such a fit of coughing that he was compelled to leave the room for a time, arousing bewilderment in everyone present.

In short, all was clear. Maria Alexandrovna realised that her guests knew absolutely everything and had gathered with the very worst intentions. It was a dangerous situation. They might distract, muddle the feeble-minded old man right there in her presence. They might even take the Prince away from her, making him fall out with her this very evening and luring him away with them. Anything was to be expected. But fate was preparing one more ordeal for her: the door opened and there was Mozglyakov, whom she had thought to be with Boroduyev and whom she had not been expecting to visit her this evening at all. She winced as if something had pricked her.

Mozglyakov stopped in the doorway and, a little flustered, surveyed everyone. He was quite unable to cope with the agitation which was clearly written on his face.

'Ah, good heavens! Pavel Alexandrovich!' cried several voices.

'Ah, good heavens! But it is Pavel Alexandrovich! How is it, Maria Alexandrovna, that you said he'd gone to see Boroduyev? We were told you'd gone into hiding at Boroduyev's, Pavel Alexandrovich,' squeaked Natalya Dmitriyevna.

'Gone into hiding?' repeated Mozglyakov with a distorted sort of smile. 'A strange expression! Forgive me, Natalya Dmitriyevna! I'm not hiding from anyone myself, and I don't want to hide anyone else,' he added with a highly meaningful glance at Maria Alexandrovna.

Maria Alexandrovna began to tremble.

'What, surely this blockhead isn't rebelling as well?' she thought, peering searchingly at Mozglyakov. 'No, that really will be worse than anything…'

'Is it true, Pavel Alexandrovich, that you've been retired… from work, it stands to reason?' the impertinent Felisata Mikhailovna made a sally, looking him mockingly straight in the eyes.

'Retired? What do you mean, retired? I'm simply changing my job. I'm getting a position in St Petersburg,' Mozglyakov replied dryly.

'Well, I congratulate you then,' Felisata Mikhailovna continued, 'we were even worried when we heard you were chasing after a position here in Mordasov. Positions here are insecure, Pavel Alexandrovich, you're likely to go flying straight away.'

'Except, perhaps, for teachers' positions in the district college; you can still find a vacancy there,' remarked Natalya Dmitriyevna. The allusion was so clear and crude that an embarrassed Anna Nikolayevna gave her venomous friend a nudge with her foot.

'Surely you don't think Pavel Alexandrovich would agree to take the position of some wretched teacher?' Felisata Mikhailovna interposed.

But Pavel Alexandrovich could find no answer. He turned and collided with Afanasy Matveyich, who was reaching out his hand to him. Mozglyakov very foolishly refused to take his hand and bowed to him mockingly from the waist. Irritated in the extreme, he went straight up to Zina and, looking her maliciously in the eye, whispered:

'This is all thanks to you. You wait, I'll show you this very evening whether or not I'm a fool.'

'Why put it off? It's obvious even now,' Zina replied loudly, sizing her former suitor up with repugnance.

Mozglyakov hurriedly turned away, alarmed by her loud voice.

'Have you come from Boroduyev?' Maria Alexandrovna finally made up her mind to ask.

'No, ma'am, I've come from my uncle.'

'Your uncle? So you've just been with the Prince, then?'

'Ah, good heavens! So the Prince is already awake, then; and we were told he was still asleep,' added Natalya Dmitriyevna, throwing venomous looks at Maria Alexandrovna.

'Don't worry about the Prince, Natalya Dmitriyevna,' replied Mozglyakov, 'he's woken up and, thank God, is already in his right mind now. He was got tipsy a little while ago, first with you, and then, on this occasion completely, here, so that he was on the point of quite losing his head, which is rather weak anyway. But now, thank God, we've had a talk together, and he's started reasoning sensibly. He'll be here in a moment to take his leave of you, Maria Alexandrovna, and to thank you for all your hospitality. At first light tomorrow we're setting off together for the hermitage, and then I myself will be sure to see him to Dukhanovo to avoid any more falls like, for example, today's; and there he'll be taken over personally by Stepanida Matveyevna, who will definitely have returned from Moscow by then, and who won't let him out to go travelling a second time, not for anything – I answer for that.'

As he said this, Mozglyakov looked maliciously at Mari Alexandrovna. The latter sat as though dumb with astonishment. With sorrow I admit that perhaps for the first time in her life my heroine had got cold feet.

'So they're leaving tomorrow at first light? But how's that, ma'am?' said Natalya Dmitriyevna, turning to Maria Alexandrovna.

'How can it be so?' rang out naively amongst the guests. 'But we'd heard... that really is strange!'

Their hostess simply didn't know what to reply. But suddenly the attention of all was diverted in the most extraordinary and eccentric way. A strange sort of noise and somebody's abrupt exclamations were heard in the next room, then suddenly, quite unexpectedly, into Maria Alexandrovna's salon burst Sofia Petrovna Farpukhina. Sofia Petrovna was unarguably the most eccentric lady in Mordasov, so eccentric that even in Mordasov it had recently been decided not to accept her into society. It should also be noted that every evening, at exactly seven o'clock, she regularly had a bite to eat – for her stomach, as she put it – and after her snack was usually in the most emancipated humour, to say the least. She was in precisely that humour now, as she burst in so unexpectedly on Maria Alexandrovna.

'Ah, so this is the way, Maria Alexandrovna,' she cried for the whole room to hear, 'this is the way you treat me! Don't worry, I've only come for a moment; I won't even sit down here. I dropped in especially to find out if what I'd been told was true. Ah! So you have balls, banquets, betrothals, and Sofia Petrovna can sit at home knitting a stocking! The whole town's invited, but not me! And a little while ago I was your friend and *mon ange*, when I came to pass on what they were doing with the Prince at Natalya Dmitriyevna's. And now here's Natalya Dmitriyevna, who you were calling every name under the sun a little while ago, and who was calling you names too, sitting here as your guest. Don't worry, Natalya Dmitriyevna! I don't want your chocolate *à la santé*[54] at ten kopeks a bar. I treat myself to a drink at home more often than you do! Pah!'

'That's obvious, ma'am,' remarked Natalya Dmitriyevna.

'But for pity's sake, Sofia Petrovna,' cried Maria Alexandrovna, flushing in annoyance, 'what's the matter with you? Do at least come to your senses.'

'Don't worry about me, Maria Alexandrovna, I know everything, I've found out everything, everything!' cried Sofia Petrovna in her abrupt, shrill voice, surrounded by all the guests, who seemed to be enjoying this unexpected scene. 'I've found out everything! Your own Nastasya came running to me and told me everything. You picked up that wretched Prince, got him drunk, made him propose to your daughter, who absolutely no one wants to marry any more, and now you think you've become a big shot – a duchess in lace – pah! Don't worry, I'm a colonel's wife myself! I couldn't care less if you didn't invite me to the betrothal! I've known people rather superior to you. I've dined with Countess Zalikhvatskaya; Chief Commissar Kurochkin wanted to marry me! I really need your invitation, don't I, pah!'

'You see, Sofia Petrovna,' answered Maria Alexandrovna, losing control of herself, 'I can assure you that people just don't go bursting into a noble home like this, and in *such a state* what's more, and if you don't rid me of your presence and eloquence at once, then I'll take my own measures straight away.'

'I know, you'll order your wretched servants to lead me out! Don't worry, I'll find the way for myself. Farewell, marry off whoever you like, and you, Natalya Dmitriyevna, kindly don't laugh at me; I couldn't care less about your chocolate! I may not have been invited here, but at least I haven't danced the kazachok in front of any princes. And what are you laughing for, Anna Nikolayevna? Sushilov's broken his leg; he's just been taken home, pah! And if you, Felisata Mikhailovna, don't order your bare-footed Matryoshka to drive your cow home in good time so that it doesn't moo outside my windows every day, then I'll break your Matryoshka's legs. Farewell, Maria Alexandrovna, lots of luck, pah!' Sofia Petrovna disappeared. The guests laughed. Maria Alexandrovna was extremely embarrassed.

'I think she's had a drink,' pronounced Natalya Dmitriyevna sweetly.

'But what audacity!'

'*Quelle abominable femme!*'[55]

'She made me laugh so!'

'Oh, the unseemly things she was saying!'

'Only what was it she was saying about a betrothal? What betrothal?' asked Felisata Mikhailovna mockingly.

'But it's dreadful!' Maria Alexandrovna finally burst out. 'These are the monsters who scatter all these absurd rumours about by the handful! The surprising thing, Felisata Mikhailovna, isn't that such ladies can be found in the midst of our society – no, the most surprising thing of all is the fact that some need is felt for these ladies, they're listened to, they're supported, they're believed, they're…'

'Prince! Prince!' all the guests suddenly cried.

'Oh, good heavens! *Ce cher prince!*'

'Well, thank God! Now we'll find out all the ins and outs,' whispered Felisata Mikhailovna to her neighbour.

CHAPTER XIII

The Prince came in and smiled sweetly. All the alarm that Mozglyakov had aroused in his chicken's heart a quarter of an hour before vanished at the sight of the ladies. He melted at once like a sweet. The ladies greeted him with a shrill cry of joy. Generally speaking, the ladies always treated our old man affectionately and were extremely unceremonious with him. He had the capacity to amuse them with his person to an unbelievable extent. Felisata Mikhailovna had even averred in the morning (not seriously, of course) that she was prepared to sit on his knees if he found it pleasant, 'because he's ever such a nice old man, endlessly nice!' Maria Alexandrovna fastened her eyes upon him, wanting to read at least something in his face and to have a way out of her critical position ready. It was clear that Mozglyakov had played a terribly dirty trick and that her entire venture was wobbling violently. But nothing could be read in the Prince's face. He was the same as he had been a little while before, as he always was.

'Ah, good heavens! And here's the Prince! We've been waiting and waiting for you,' cried some of the ladies.

'Impatiently, Prince, impatiently!' squeaked others.

'That's extremely fla-ttering for me,' lisped the Prince, sitting down at the table on which the samovar was boiling. The ladies surrounded him at once. Only Anna Nikolayevna and Natalya Dmitriyevna remained beside Maria Alexandrovna. Afanasy Matveyich was smiling deferentially. Mozglyakov was smiling too, and gazing with a defiant air at Zina who, without paying him the slightest attention, went over to her father and sat down beside him in an armchair by the fireplace.

'Ah, Prince, is it true what they're saying, that you're leaving us?' squeaked Felisata Mikhailovna.

'Why yes, *mesdames*, I'm leaving. I want to go a-broad im-me-diately.'

'Abroad, Prince, abroad!' they all exclaimed as one. 'But why have you taken that idea into your head?'

'A-broad,' the Prince confirmed, preening himself, 'and, do you know, I particularly want to go there for the new i-deas.'

'What does that mean, for the new ideas? What's that about?' said the ladies, exchanging looks with one another.

'Why yes, for the new ideas,' the Prince repeated with an air of the deepest conviction. 'Everyone goes for the new ideas now. And I want to get the new i-deas too.'

'You don't want to join a Masonic lodge, do you, dearest Uncle?' Mozglyakov interpolated, evidently wanting to show off his wit and familiarity in front of the ladies.

'Why yes, my friend, you're not mistaken,' his uncle unexpectedly replied. 'I did in-deed in olden times be-long to a Masonic lodge abroad and in my turn even had very many magnanimous ideas. I even intended at the time to do a lot for con-tem-po-rary enlight-enment, and in Frankfurt was right on the point of leaving my Sidor, whom I'd taken abroad with me with the aim of setting him free. But to my surprise he ran away from me himself. He was an extremely strange per-son. Then all of a sudden I meet him in Pa-ris, such a dandy, with side-whiskers, walking down a boulevard with a mamselle. He glanced at me, no-dded his head. And the mamselle with him was so spry and bright-eyed, so a-llu-ring…'

'Why, Uncle! After that, you'll be setting all the peasants free if you go abroad now!' exclaimed Mozglyakov, guffawing for all he was worth.

'You've guessed my wishes completely, my dear,' replied the Prince without hesitation. 'I do indeed mean to set them all free.'

'But for pity's sake, Prince, I mean, they'll all run away from you at once, and then who will there be to pay you quit-rent?' exclaimed Felisata Mikhailovna.

'Of course they'll all scatter,' responded Anna Nikolayevna in alarm.

'Oh, good heavens! Will they rea-lly run away?' exclaimed the Prince in surprise.

'They will, sir, they'll run away at once, sir, and they'll leave you on your own, sir,' Natalya Dmitriyevna confirmed.

'Oh, good heavens! Well, then I won't set them free. Anyway, it was just talk, you know.'

'It's better that way, Uncle,' Mozglyakov gave his endorsement.

Up until now Maria Alexandrovna had been listening in silence and observing. It seemed to her that the Prince had completely forgotten about her, and that this was not at all natural.

'Permit me, Prince,' she began loudly and with dignity, 'to introduce my husband, Afanasy Matveyich, to you. He came back from the country especially, as soon as he heard that you'd put up at my house.'

Afanasy Matveyich smiled and assumed a dignified air. He thought he had been praised.

'Ah, I'm very pleased to meet you,' said the Prince, 'A-fa-nasy Matveyich! Permit me, I'm re-mem-bering something. A-fa-nasy Mat-vey-ich. Why yes, he's the one who's in the country. *Charmant, charmant*, I'm very pleased to meet you. My friend,' exclaimed the Prince, turning to Mozglyakov, 'it's that very man, isn't it, you remember, earlier on it came out in rhyme. How did it go? The husband's off, and the wife… why yes, the wife's gone to some town or other too…'

'Ah, Prince, it must be "The husband's off, and the wife's in Tambov", that vaudeville which the actors put on here last year,' Felisata Mikhailovna chimed in.

'Why yes, in Tambov, precisely; I forget e-ver-ything. *Charmant, charmant*! So you are that very man? I'm extremely pleased to meet you,' said the Prince, reaching out a hand to the smiling Afanasy Matveyich without getting up from his armchair. 'Well, how's your health?'

'Hm…'

'He's well, Prince, well,' Maria Alexandrovna replied hurriedly.

'Why yes, it's quite evident that he's well. And you're still in the coun-try? Well, I'm very pleased to meet you. How ro-sy-cheeked he is, and forever laughing…'

Afanasy Matveyich was smiling, bowing, and even scraping his feet. But at the Prince's last remark he couldn't restrain himself and suddenly, for no reason at all, he burst out laughing in the silliest manner. Everyone roared with laughter. The ladies squealed with delight. Zina blushed and looked with flashing eyes at Maria Alexandrovna who, in her turn, was exploding with fury. It was time to change the subject.

'How did you sleep, Prince?' she asked in a honeyed voice, at the same time letting Afanasy Matveyich know with a threatening look that he should clear off back to his place at once.

'Oh, I slept very well,' the Prince responded, 'and do you know, I had an enchan-ting dream, an en-chan-ting dream!'

'A dream! I really love it when people talk about their dreams,' exclaimed Felisata Mikhailovna.

'And so do I, sir, I really love it, sir!' added Natalya Dmitriyevna.

'An en-chan-ting dream,' the Prince repeated with a sweet smile, 'but at the same time, the dream is the grea-test secret!'

'What, Prince, can it really not be told? It must be an amazing sort of dream, then?' remarked Anna Nikolayevna.

'The grea-test secret,' the Prince repeated, egging the curious ladies on with delight.

'Well, it must be terribly interesting!' cried the ladies.

'I bet the Prince was kneeling before some beauty in his dream and making a declaration of love!' exclaimed Felisata Mikhailovna. 'Well, Prince, admit that it's true! Admit it, dear Prince!'

'Admit it, Prince, admit it!' they joined in on all sides.

The Prince heeded all these cries solemnly and ecstatically. The ladies' suggestions were extremely flattering to his self-esteem, and he was all but smacking his lips.

'Although I did say that my dream was the greatest secret,' he finally replied, 'I am forced to confess that, to my surprise, madams, you have guessed almost com-pletely right.'

'I guessed right!' exclaimed Felisata Mikhailovna in rapture. 'Well, Prince! Say whatever you like now, you have to tell us who your beauty is.'

'You must tell us!'

'A local girl, or not?'

'Tell us, dear Prince.'

'Darling Prince, tell us! No matter what, tell us!' they cried on all sides.

'*Mesdames, mesdames*!… if you are so very in-sis-tent about wanting to know, then I can tell you just one thing, that she is the most en-chan-ting and, one might say, the most chaste maiden of all that I know,' mumbled the utterly molten Prince.

'The most enchanting! And… a local! Who could it be?' the ladies asked, exchanging meaningful looks and winks with one another.

'It stands to reason, she that's considered our leading beauty,' said Natalya Dmitriyevna, rubbing her huge red hands and throwing glances at Zina with her feline eyes. And everyone looked, along with her, at Zina.

'But how's that, Prince, if you have such dreams, then why not get married in reality?' asked Felisata Mikhailovna, looking around at everyone meaningfully.

'What a marvellous wedding we'd give you!' a second lady chimed in.

'Dear Prince, do get married!' squeaked a third.

'Get married, get married!' they cried on all sides. 'Why not get married?'

'Why yes… why not get married?' the Prince yielded, muddled by all these cries.

'Uncle!' exclaimed Mozglyakov.

'Why yes, my friend, I un-der-stand you! That's just what I wanted to tell you, *mesdames*, that I'm no longer fit to get married, and after spending an enchan-ting evening with our charming hostess, I'm setting off tomorrow for Father Misail's hermitage, and then going directly abroad to keep up more easily with Euro-pean en-ligh-tenment.'

Zina turned pale and looked at her mother in inexpressible anguish. But Maria Alexandrovna had already made up her mind. Until now she had just been biding her time, testing things out, although she had realised they had gone very wrong and that her enemies had left her a very long way behind on the road. Finally she had understood everything and had made up her mind, in one go, with one blow, to smash the hundred-headed hydra. She rose grandly from her armchair and approached the table with a firm tread, measuring her pygmy enemies with a proud gaze. In that gaze shone the fire of inspiration. She had made up her mind to stun all these poisonous gossips, to throw them into confusion, to crush that good-for-nothing Mozglyakov like a cockroach, and with one decisive, bold blow to regain all her lost influence over that idiot of a Prince. It stands to reason, extraordinary audacity was demanded; but Maria Alexandrovna had never been short of audacity!

'*Mesdames*,' she began solemnly and with dignity (Maria Alexandrovna was, in general, extremely fond of solemnity), '*mesdames*, I've been listening for a long time to your conversation, to your merry and witty jokes, and find that it's time for me to have my say. You know we've all gathered together here completely by chance (and I'm so glad of it, so glad)… Never would I have been first to resolve to tell an important family secret or to disclose it earlier than is demanded by the most ordinary sense of decorum. In particular I beg forgiveness of my dear guest; but it seemed to me that, with his little allusions to the same fact, he himself was giving me the idea that not only would the formal and solemn announcement of our family secret not be displeasing for him, but that he even desired the disclosure… Isn't that so, Prince, I wasn't mistaken?'

'Why no, you weren't mistaken… and I'm very, very glad…' said the Prince, not understanding what was going on at all.

Maria Alexandrovna paused to draw breath for greater effect, and looked round at the entire company. All the guests were listening intently to her words with greedy and anxious curiosity. Mozglyakov winced; Zina turned red and half-rose from her chair; Afanasy Matveyich, in expectation of something extraordinary, and just to be on the safe side, blew his nose.

'Yes, *mesdames*, it is with joy that I am prepared to entrust you with my family secret. After lunch today, the Prince, carried away by the beauty and… the virtues of my daughter, did her the honour of proposing. Prince!' she concluded in a voice tremulous with tears and agitation, 'dear Prince, you must not, you cannot be angry with me for my indiscretion! Only the extreme joy of the family could have torn this dear secret prematurely from my heart, and… what mother can blame me in this instance?'

I cannot find the words to depict the impact made by Maria Alexandrovna's unexpected outburst. It was as if everyone had frozen in astonishment. The perfidious guests, who had thought to alarm Maria Alexandrovna by prior knowledge of her secret, who had thought to finish her off by the premature revelation of that secret, who had thought to harrow her with, for the moment, just hints alone, were stupefied by such bold candour. Such fearless candour was a sign of strength.

'So the Prince really is, of his own free will, going to marry Zina? So he wasn't lured, he wasn't made to drink too much, he wasn't duped? So he isn't being forced to get married in a secretive, furtive way? So Maria Alexandrovna's afraid of no one? So the wedding can't be called off now, if the Prince isn't getting married under duress?' A momentary whispering was heard, which turned suddenly into shrill cries of joy. The first to rush to embrace Maria Alexandrovna was Natalya Dmitriyevna; after her was Anna Nikolayevna, after her Felisata Mikhailovna. Everyone leapt up from their seats, everyone mingled. Many of the ladies were pale with rage. They began congratulating an embarrassed Zina; they even caught hold of Afanasy Matveyich. Maria Alexandrovna held out her arms in picturesque fashion and, almost by force, enfolded her daughter in an embrace. The Prince alone looked at the whole scene with a strange sort of surprise, although he was smiling as before. Actually, he did in part find the scene pleasing. At the embrace of mother and daughter he took out his handkerchief and wiped his eyes, in which little tears had appeared. It stands to reason, the ladies rushed to him with their congratulations too.

'Congratulations, Prince! Congratulations!' they cried on all sides.

'So you're getting married?'

'So you really are getting married?'

'Dear Prince, so you're getting married?'

'Why yes, why yes,' the Prince replied, extremely happy with the congratulations and delight, 'and I admit to you that I'm pleased more than anything by your sweet fellow-feeling for me, which I shall ne-ver forget, ne-ver forget. *Charmant! Charmant!* You've even made me shed a tear…'

'Kiss me, Prince!' cried Felisata Mikhailovna, louder than anyone.

'And, I admit to you,' the Prince continued, being interrupted from all sides, 'I'm surprised most of all at the way Maria Iva-no-vna, our estee-med hostess, has with such extraor-dinary perspicacity divined my dream. Just as if *she* had had it in-stead of me. Extraor-dinary perspicacity! Ex-tra-or-dinary perspicacity!'

'Oh, Prince, are you on about that dream again?'

'Come on, own up, Prince, own up!' everyone cried, clustering around him.

'Yes, Prince, concealment's no use, it's time to reveal the secret,' said Maria Alexandrovna decisively and sternly. 'I understood your subtle allegory, the enchanting delicacy with which you tried to hint to me of your desire to make your courtship public. Yes, *mesdames*, it's true: the Prince knelt before my daughter today, and, in real life, not in a dream, solemnly proposed to her.'

'Exactly as though in real life, and even in those very circumstances,' the Prince confirmed. '*Mademoiselle*,' he continued, turning with extraordinary politeness to Zina, who had still not recovered from her astonishment, '*Mademoiselle*! I swear that I would never have dared to pronounce your name if others had not pro-nounced it before me. It was an enchanting dream, an en-chan-ting dream, and I am doubly happy that I have now been permitted to tell you so. *Charmant*! *Charmant*!…'

'But, forgive me, what's going on? He's still talking about a dream, isn't he,' whispered Anna Nikolayevna to the alarmed and somewhat pale Maria Alexandrovna. Alas! Even without these warnings, there had already for some time been an ache and palpitations in Maria Alexandrovna's heart.

'What's going on?' whispered the ladies, exchanging glances with one another.

'Forgive me, Prince,' Maria Alexandrovna began with a painfully contorted smile, 'I assure you that you amaze me. What's this strange idea you have about a dream? I admit to you, up until now I thought you were joking, but… If this is a joke, then it's a rather inappropriate one… I want to, I'd like to ascribe it to your absentmindedness, but…'

'Indeed, ma'am, perhaps it's because of his absentmindedness,' hissed Natalya Dmitriyevna.

'Why yes… perhaps it is because of absentmin-dedness,' the Prince confirmed, still without entirely understanding what was wanted of him. 'And imagine, I'll relate an a-nec-dote to you now. I'm invited, in St Petersburg, to a fu-neral, to these people, *maison bourgeoise, mais honnête*,[56] but I went and mixed things up, thinking it was to a name-day party. The name-day party had ta-ken place just the week be-fore. I prepared a bouquet of camellias for the lady. I go in, and what do I see? A venerable, respectable man lying on the table, and so how asto-nished I was. I simply didn't know where to put myself with the bou-quet.'

'But Prince, this isn't a matter of anecdotes!' Maria Alexandrovna interrupted in vexation. 'My daughter has no need to chase after suitors, of course, but a little while ago, you yourself, here, by this grand piano, proposed to her. I didn't provoke you into it… You might say that it shocked me… It stands to reason, just one thought came to mind, and I put everything off until you woke up. But I'm a mother; she is my daughter… You were talking about some sort of dream just now, and I thought you wanted, in the guise of an allegory, to tell of your engagement. I know very well that people may be trying to confuse you… I even suspect precisely who… but… explain yourself, Prince, explain yourself quickly, properly. You can't joke like this with a noble house.'

'Why no, you can't joke like this with a noble house,' the Prince involuntarily assented, but already starting, little by little, to get worried.

'But that isn't a response to my question, Prince. I'm asking you to give a positive response; confirm, confirm here and now, in front of everyone, that a little while ago you proposed to my daughter.'

'Why yes, I'm prepared to confirm it. I've already related it all though, and Felisata Yakovlevna completely divined my dream.'

'Not a dream! Not a dream!' Maria Alexandrovna cried in fury, 'not a dream, it was in reality, Prince, in reality, do you hear, in reality!'

'In reality!' exclaimed the Prince, rising from his chair in surprise. 'Well, my friend, as you prophesied a little while ago, this is how it's turned out!' he added, turning to Mozglyakov. 'But I can assure you, esteemed Maria Stepanovna, that you're deluded! I'm absolutely certain that I only dreamt about it!'

'Lord, have mercy!' Maria Alexandrovna cried out.

'Don't grieve, Maria Alexandrovna,' Natalya Dmitriyevna took her part. 'Maybe the Prince has somehow forgotten. He'll remember.'

'I'm surprised at you, Natalya Dmitriyevna,' retorted Maria Alexandrovna in indignation, 'do such things really get forgotten? Can it really be forgotten? For pity's sake, Prince, are you mocking us, or what? Or perhaps you're posing as one of those idlers of the time of the regency depicted by Dumas? Some Fairelacour, Lauzun?[57] But besides the fact that at your age it's unbecoming, I can assure you that you won't succeed! My daughter isn't a French viscountess. A little while ago,

125

here, right here, she sang you a romance, and carried away by her singing, you dropped to your knees and proposed to her. I'm not dreaming, am I? I'm not asleep, am I? Speak, Prince: am I asleep or not?'

'Why yes… but then, perhaps not…' replied the bewildered Prince. 'I mean to say that I don't seem to be asleep now. A little while ago, you see, I was asleep, and so I had a dream, which was while I was asleep…'

'My word, good heavens, what is this all about: not asleep – asleep, asleep – not asleep! The Devil knows what it's all about! Are you raving, Prince, or what?'

'Why yes, the Devil knows… but I seem to be completely muddled now…' said the Prince, throwing anxious looks all around.

'But how could you have dreamt it,' Maria Alexandrovna lamented, 'when I'm recounting to you in such detail your very own dream, when you haven't yet recounted it to any of us?'

'But maybe the Prince has already recounted it to somebody,' said Natalya Dmitriyevna.

'Why yes, maybe I have recounted it to somebody,' confirmed the totally flustered Prince.

'Here's a comedy!' whispered Felisata Mikhailovna to her neighbour.

'Oh good heavens! Anyone's patience would run out at this!' cried Maria Alexandrovna, wringing her hands in a frenzy. 'She sang you a romance, a romance she sang you! Dream that as well, did you?'

'Why yes, she did indeed seem to sing a romance,' the Prince mumbled pensively, and suddenly his face was enlivened by some sort of memory. 'My friend,' he exclaimed, turning to Mozglyakov, 'I forgot to tell you a little while ago that there truly was a romance, and there were castles of some sort all the time in the romance, and so there was a huge number of castles, and then there was some sort of troubadour! Why yes, I remember it all… and so I even started crying… And now I'm having difficulty, as though it did actually happen, and wasn't a dream…'

'I admit to you, Uncle,' replied Mozglyakov as calmly as he could, although his voice was trembling with some sort of alarm, 'I admit to you, I think this can all be very easily settled and reconciled. I think you did indeed hear singing. Zinaida Afanasyevna sings beautifully. You were brought here after lunch, and Zinaida Afanasyevna sang you a romance. I wasn't here then, but you were probably deeply moved and remembered the old days; perhaps you remembered that Viscountess with whom you yourself once sang romances and of whom you were telling us yourself this morning. Well, and then, when you went to bed, in consequence of the pleasant impressions, you dreamt you were in love and proposing...'

Maria Alexandrovna was simply stunned by such audacity.

'Ah, my friend, you know, that is indeed the way it was,' cried the Prince in delight. 'In consequence of the pleasant impressions, precisely! I do indeed remember having a romance sung to me, and that was why, while I was asleep, I wanted to get married. And there was the Viscountess too... Ah, how cleverly you've puzzled it out, my friend! Well! Now I'm absolutely certain that I dreamt it all! Maria Vasilyevna! I assure you, you're mistaken! It was a dream. Otherwise I couldn't possibly have played with your noble feelings...'

'Ah! I can see clearly now who's done the dirty here!' cried Maria Alexandrovna, beside herself with fury and turning to Mozglyakov. 'It's you, sir, you, you dishonourable man, you that's done it all! You've stirred up this wretched idiot because you yourself have been refused! But you'll pay me for this injury you loathsome man! You'll pay, you'll pay, you'll pay!'

'Maria Alexandrovna,' cried Mozglyakov in his turn, becoming as red as a lobster, 'your words are to such a degree... I really don't know to what degree your words are... There's not a single society lady would allow herself... At least I'm protecting my relative. You must agree, luring him like that...'

'Why yes, luring me like that...' agreed the Prince, trying to hide behind Mozglyakov.

'Afanasy Matveyich!' Maria Alexandrovna shrieked in an unnatural sort of voice. 'Can't you hear the way we're being shamed and dishonoured? Or have you completely given up any sort of responsibility now? Or are you indeed not the head of a family, but a repulsive wooden post? What are you looking blank for? Any other husband would have long ago washed away the injury to his family with blood!...'

'Wife!' Afanasy Matveyich began pompously, proud that a need had arisen even for him, 'Wife! Didn't *you* indeed actually dream all of this, and then, when you woke, go and muddle everything up to accord with your version…'

But Afanasy Matveyich was not destined to complete his sharp-witted conjecture. Until now the guests had been restraining themselves and craftily adopting an air of proper seriousness of sorts. But at this point a loud salvo of the most unrestrained laughter filled the entire room. Forgetting all the proprieties, Maria Alexandrovna was about to rush at her spouse, probably with a view to scratching his eyes out at once. But she was forcibly restrained. Natalya Dmitriyevna exploited the circumstances and, albeit only a little drop, did still add some more poison.

'Ah, Maria Alexandrovna, perhaps that really is the way it was, ma'am, and here you are upsetting yourself,' she said in the most honeyed voice.

'What way? What was?' cried Maria Alexandrovna, not yet under-standing properly.

'Ah, Maria Alexandrovna, it can sometimes happen, you know…'

'What can happen? Are you trying to plague the life out of me, or something?'

'Perhaps you really did dream it.'

'Dream it? Me? Dream it? And you dare to say that straight to my face?'

'Well, perhaps that really is the way it was,' responded Felisata Mikhailovna.

'Why yes, perhaps that really is the way it was,' the Prince mumbled too.

'And him, he's at it too! Lord God!' Maria Alexandrovna exclaimed, clasping her hands together.

'How you do upset yourself, Maria Alexandrovna! Do remember, ma'am, that dreams are sent down by God. Now if God desires something, then it's no one but God's desire, ma'am, and His holy will lies upon everything. There's absolutely no point getting angry about it, ma'am.'

'Why no, no point getting angry,' agreed the Prince.

'Do you take me for a madwoman, or something?' Maria Alexandrovna barely managed to articulate as she choked with rage. This was already beyond human strength. She hastened to find a chair and fell into a faint. A commotion arose.

'It's out of politeness, ma'am, that she's fallen into a faint,' Natalya Dmitriyevna whispered to Anna Nikolayevna.

But at that moment, the moment when the bewilderment of the audience and tension of the entire scene were at their height, there suddenly came forward a hitherto speechless character – and the nature of the entire scene immediately altered…

CHAPTER XIV

Zinaida Afanasyevna was, generally speaking, extremely romantic by nature. We don't know if it was because, as Maria Alexandrovna herself asserted, she had read too much of 'that fool' Shakespeare with 'her wretched teacher', but never yet, in all her life in Mordasov, had Zina permitted herself such an extraordinarily romantic, or, to put it better, heroic outburst as the one we are now going to describe.

Pale, with resolution in her gaze yet almost trembling with agitation, and wonderfully beautiful in her indignation, she stepped forward. Casting a long, defiant gaze at everyone, she turned, in the midst of the silence that suddenly fell, to her mother, who, at Zina's first movement, had immediately come round from her faint and opened her eyes.

'Mamma!' said Zina. 'Why try to deceive? Why besmirch yourself with lies as well? Everything's already so dirty by now that, truly, it isn't worth the humiliating trouble of covering up the dirt!'

'Zina! Zina! What's the matter with you? Pull yourself together!' exclaimed the frightened Maria Alexandrovna, leaping up from her armchair…

'I told you, I told you beforehand, Mamma, that I couldn't endure all this shame,' Zina continued. 'Is it really absolutely necessary to humiliate oneself even more, to sully oneself even more? But you should know, Mamma, that I'll take everything upon myself, because I'm more to blame than anyone. I, I by my consent set this vile… intrigue in motion! You're my mother; you love me; you thought in your own way, according to your own notions, to arrange my happiness. You at least can be forgiven; but I, I – never!'

'Zina, surely you don't mean to tell?… Oh God! I had a premonition that this dagger wouldn't pass my heart by!'

'Yes, Mamma, I'm going to tell everything! I'm disgraced, you… we're all disgraced!…'

'You're exaggerating, Zina! You're beside yourself and you don't realise what you're saying! And why ever tell? There's no sense in it… There's no shame on us… I'll prove right now that there's no shame on us…'

'No, Mamma,' Zina exclaimed with an angry tremor in her voice, 'I don't want to be silent any longer in front of these people whose opinion I despise and who came here to mock us! I don't want to endure insults from them; not one of them has the right to throw dirt at me. All of them are ready to behave thirty times worse than you or I right now! Do they dare, are they able to be our judges?'

'That's lovely! How's that for a start! What's this! We're the ones being insulted!' was heard from all sides.

'She really doesn't understand what she's saying,' said Natalya Dmitriyevna.

We'll note in parenthesis that what Natalya Dmitriyevna said was justified. If Zina didn't consider these ladies worthy to judge her, why ever did she address them with such openness, with such admissions? In general, Zinaida Afanasyevna was extremely hasty. Such was the subsequent opinion of the very best heads in Mordasov. Everything could have been put right! Everything could have been settled! True, Maria Alexandrovna ruined things for herself too that evening with her haste and arrogance. All that was needed was to have a good laugh at the idiotic old man and to throw him out! But, as if deliberately, contrary to common sense and Mordasovan wisdom, Zina turned to the Prince.

'Prince,' she said to the old man, who even half-rose from his chair out of respect, so smitten was he by her at that moment. 'Prince! Forgive me, forgive us! We deceived, we lured you…'

'Will you be quiet, you wretched girl!' Maria Alexandrovna exclaimed in a frenzy.

'Madam! Madam! *Ma charmante enfant*…' mumbled the smitten Prince.

But Zina's proud, impulsive and in the highest degree dreamy nature was at that moment carrying her away from the sphere of all the proprieties demanded by reality. She had forgotten even about her mother, who was contorting convulsively at her admissions.

'Yes, we both deceived you, Prince; Mamma by resolving to force you to marry me, and I by agreeing to it. You were given wine to get you drunk, I agreed to sing and curry favour with you. Weak, defenceless, you were *bamboozled*, as Pavel Alexandrovich put it, bamboozled because of your wealth, because of your being a prince. It was all terribly base, and I repent of it. But I swear to you, Prince, that I resolved upon this base deed not out of any base motive. I wanted... But what am I doing! It's doubly base to try and justify yourself in such a matter! But I declare to you, Prince, that had I taken anything from you, then in return I would have been your plaything, servant, dancer, slave... I swore to it and would have kept my vow religiously!...'

A powerful spasm in her throat stopped her at that moment. It was as if all the guests had frozen, and they were listening wide-eyed. Zina's unexpected and utterly incomprehensible outburst had confused them. The Prince alone was moved to tears, although he had not understood even half of what Zina had said.

'But I'll marry you, *ma belle enfant*, if you de-sire it so,' he mumbled, 'and it will be a great ho-nour for me! Only I assure you that it rea-lly did seem to be a dream... Well, I dream about all sorts of things, don't I? Why get so an-xious? I don't even seem to have understood anything, *mon ami*,' he continued, turning to Mozglyakov, 'won't you at least explain things to me, please...'

'And you, Pavel Alexandrovich,' Zina chimed in, turning to Mozglyakov as well, 'you, upon whom I had at one time practically resolved to look as my future husband, you, who have now so cruelly avenged yourself upon me – could you too really have joined with these people to torment and disgrace me? And you said that you loved me! But I'm not the one to lecture you on morals! I'm guiltier than you. I've insulted you, because I really did entice you with promises, and my arguments a little earlier were all lies and cunning! I never loved you, and if I did try to resolve upon marrying you, it was solely to get away from here, anywhere, if only away from this accursed town, and to rid myself of all this stench... But, I swear to you, upon marrying you, I would have been a good and faithful wife to you... You've avenged yourself upon me cruelly and, if it flatters your pride...'

'Zinaida Afanasyevna!' Mozglyakov exclaimed.

'If you still harbour hatred towards me...'

'Zinaida Afanasyevna!'

'If ever,' Zina continued, quelling the tears within her, 'if ever you loved me...'

'Zinaida Afanasyevna!'

'Zina, Zina! My daughter!' wailed Maria Alexandrovna.

'I'm a cad, Zinaida Afanasyevna, I'm a cad and nothing more!' Mozglyakov confirmed, and everything became most terribly agitated. Cries of amazement and indignation arose, but Mozglyakov stood rooted to the ground, without a thought and without a voice…

For weak and shallow natures accustomed to constant subordination, but then finally resolving on flying into a rage and protesting, resolving, in short, on being firm and consistent, there is always a boundary – the nearby limit of their firmness and consistency. At first their protest is usually most energetic. Their energy even reaches the point of frenzy. They hurl themselves at obstacles with their eyes screwed up, as it were, and almost always shoulder a burden beyond their powers. But it is as if, upon reaching a certain point, the enraged person suddenly takes fright at himself and stops, stupefied, with the terrible question: 'What ever have I done?' Then he immediately goes limp, whines, demands to discuss things, kneels down, begs forgiveness, and pleads for everything to be as of old, only quickly, as quickly as possible!… It was almost the same now with Mozglyakov. Having been beside himself, having become enraged, having brought about a disaster which he now ascribed wholly to himself alone; having sated his indignation and self-esteem, and having come to hate himself for it, he suddenly stopped, conscience-stricken, in the face of Zina's unexpected outburst. Her final words finished him off completely. Skipping from one extreme to the other was a matter of a moment.

'I'm an ass, Zinaida Afanasyevna!' he exclaimed in a burst of frenzied repentance. 'No! Why an ass? An ass – that's nothing! I'm incomparably worse than an ass! But I'll prove to you, Zinaida Afanasyevna, I'll prove to you that even an ass can be a noble person!… Uncle! I deceived you! I, I deceived you! You weren't asleep; you did indeed propose in reality, and I, I, a cad, in revenge for having been refused, assured you that you'd dreamt it all.'

'Amazingly curious things are being revealed, ma'am,' hissed Natalya Dmitriyevna into Anna Nikolayevna's ear.

'My friend,' replied the Prince, 'please, calm your-self; truly, you frightened me with your cry. I assure you that you're mis-ta-ken…

I suppose I'm prepared to get married, if I really have to; but you yourself assured me, you know, that it was only a dream…'

'Oh, how can I convince you? Teach me, how am I to convince him now? Uncle, Uncle! This is an important thing, you know, the most important family matter! Understand! Think!'

'My friend, be so kind, I'll have a think. Wait, let me remember everything in or-der. First I dreamt of Fe-o-fil the coachman.'

'Oh, now's not the time for Feofil, Uncle!'

'Why no, let's say now isn't the time for him. Then there was Na-po-le-on, and then we seem to have been having tea, and some lady came and ate all our sugar…'

'But Uncle,' Mozglyakov blurted out, having a mental lapse, 'I mean, it was Maria Alexandrovna who told you that earlier on about Natalya Dmitriyevna! I was here too, you know, I heard it myself! I hid and watched you through a little hole…'

'What, Maria Alexandrovna,' Natalya Dmitriyevna chimed in, 'so you've even been telling the Prince I stole the sugar from your sugar-bowl! So I come and visit you to thieve sugar!'

'Get out of my sight!' cried Maria Alexandrovna, driven to despair.

'No, I won't, Maria Alexandrovna, don't you dare talk to me like that, ma'am; and so I steal sugar from you? I heard some time ago that you were putting out vile rumours of the sort about me. Sofia Petrovna, ma'am, told me about it in detail… So I steal sugar from you?…'

'But *mesdames*,' exclaimed the Prince, 'I mean, it was only a dream! Well, I dream about all sorts of things, don't I?…'

'Damned old bag,' muttered Maria Alexandrovna under her breath.

'What, so I'm an old bag too!' screamed Natalya Dmitriyevna. 'And what are you, ma'am? I've known for some time that you call me an old bag. I, at least I've got a husband, ma'am, whereas you've got a fool…'

'Why yes, I remember, there was an old bag too,' the Prince muttered involuntarily, remembering the conversation of a while before with Maria Alexandrovna.

'What, and you're at it too, abusing a noblewoman, sir? How dare you, Prince, abuse a noblewoman? If I'm an old bag, then you, sir, are legless…'

'Who, me, legless?'

'Why yes, sir, legless, and toothless too, sir, that's what you are, sir!'

'And one-eyed too!' cried Maria Alexandrovna.

'You've got a corset instead of ribs, sir!' added Natalya Dmitriyevna.

'A face on springs!'

'No hair of your own, sir!'

'And the fool has a false moustache too,' confirmed Maria Alexandrovna.

'Do at least leave me my real nose, Maria Stepanovna!' exclaimed the Prince, stupefied by such sudden revelations. 'My friend! It's you that have sold me! It's you that have told people my hair's false...'

'Uncle!'

'No, my friend, I can't stay here any longer now. Take me away somewhere... *quelle société!*[58] Where is it you brought me, good heavens!'

'Idiot! Scoundrel!' cried Maria Alexandrovna.

'Good heavens!' said the poor Prince. 'I've just for-gotten a li-ttle what I came here for, but I'll re-member soon. Do take me away some-where, my boy, or else I shall be torn to pieces! What's more... I need to make a note of a new idea im-me-diately...'

'Come on, Uncle, it's not yet late; I'll take you to the hotel straight away, and I'll move in there with you myself...'

'Why yes, to the ho-tel. *Adieu, ma charmante enfant*... you alone... just you alone... are vir-tuous. You're a no-ble girl! Come on then, my dear. Oh, good heavens!'

But I shan't begin to describe the conclusion of the unpleasant scene that took place upon the Prince's exit. The guests dispersed with screams and curses. Maria Alexandrovna finally remained alone, amidst the ruins and debris of her former glory. Alas! Power, glory, significance – it had all disappeared in that one evening! Maria Alexandrovna realised that she would now be unable to rise to where she had been before. Her many long years of despotic rule over the whole of society had completely collapsed. What remained for her now? To philosophise? But she didn't do that. She raged the whole night long. Zina was dishonoured, there'd be endless gossip! How awful!

As a faithful historian, I must mention that the one who bore the brunt of this hangover was Afanasy Matveyich, who finally took refuge in a lumber-room somewhere, and froze there through until morning. And the morning did finally come, but it too brought nothing good. Misfortune never comes alone…

CHAPTER XV

If fate once brings misfortune down upon a person, there's no end whatsoever to its blows. That has long been remarked. Wasn't the disgrace and shame of the day before alone enough for Maria Alexandrovna? No! Fate was preparing for her something more and something better.

Even before ten o'clock in the morning there suddenly spread through the whole town a strange and almost incredible rumour, greeted by all with the most spiteful and embittered joy – the way all of us usually greet any unusual scandal that has come upon one of our neighbours. 'To lose all shame and conscience to such a degree,' they cried on all sides, 'to demean oneself to such a degree, to disregard all the proprieties, to loosen the reins to such a degree!' and so on, and so forth.

What happened, however, was this. Early in the morning, practically before seven, a poor, pathetic old woman came running to Maria Alexandrovna's house in despair and tears and implored the housemaid to wake the young mistress as quickly as possible, just the young mistress alone, in secret, so that Maria Alexandrovna didn't somehow find out. Pale and exhausted, Zina ran out to the old woman at once. The latter fell at her feet, kissed them, spilled tears over them and beseeched Zina to go with her at once to her sick Vasya, who had been so bad all night, so bad that he might not last even one day longer. Sobbing, the old woman told Zina that Vasya himself was asking her to come to him to say goodbye in his final hour, entreating her by all the holy angels and by all that there had been before, and that if she didn't come, then he would die in despair. Zina immediately made up her mind to go, despite the fact that the fulfilment of such a request would obviously confirm all the earlier malicious rumours about the intercepted note, about her scandalous behaviour, and so on. Without informing her mother, she threw on her coat and ran off with the old woman at once, ran through the entire town to one of the poorest suburbs of Mordasov, to the most out-of-the-way street, where there stood, sunk into the ground, a wretched, ramshackle, crooked little house with something like slits instead of windows, beset on all sides by snowdrifts.

In this wretched little house, in a small, low-ceilinged and stuffy room, in which an enormous stove occupied exactly half of all the space, on an unpainted plank bed, on a straw mattress as flat as a pancake there lay a young man covered with an old greatcoat. His face was pale and emaciated, his eyes shone with an unhealthy light, his hands were thin and dry, like sticks; his breathing was difficult and hoarse. It could be discerned that he had once been good-looking; but sickness had distorted the fine features of his handsome face, which was terrible and pathetic to look at, like the face of any consumptive, or, to be more accurate, any dying man. His aged mother, who for a whole year, almost until the last hour, had been awaiting her Vasyenka's resurrection, finally saw that he wasn't long for this world. She stood over him now, broken by grief, with her arms folded, tearless, gazing at him and unable to tear her gaze away, and nonetheless unable to comprehend, although she did know it, that in a few days her beloved Vasya would be covered with frozen earth, there, under the snowdrifts, in the paupers' graveyard. But at that moment Vasya wasn't looking at her. His entire face, wasted and suffering, now radiated bliss. Finally he saw before him the one he had dreamt of for a whole year and a half, both in waking and in sleep, throughout the long, painful nights of his illness. He realised that she had forgiven him, coming to him like God's angel in his final hour. She was squeezing his hands, crying over him, smiling at him, looking at him once more with her wonderful eyes, and everything irretrievable there had been before revived anew in the soul of the dying man. Life flared up once more in his heart and, just as it was abandoning him, seemed to want to let the suffering man have a sense of how hard it is to part with it.

'Zina,' he said, 'Zinochka! Don't cry over me, don't grieve, don't be sad, don't remind me that I'm going to die soon. I shall look at you the way that I'm looking now, I shall feel that our souls are together again, that you've forgiven me, I shall kiss your hands again, like before, and perhaps I shall die without noticing death! You've grown thin, Zinochka! O my angel, how kindly you look at me! And do you remember how you used to laugh before? Do you remember... Ah, Zina, I don't beg your forgiveness, I don't even want to recall what happened, because, Zinochka, because, although you may have

140

forgiven me, I shall never forgive myself. There have been long nights, Zina, sleepless, terrible nights, and during those nights, here on this very bed, I lay for a long time thinking, thinking a great deal about many things, and decided long ago that it was better for me to die, honest to God, better!... I wasn't suited for living, Zinochka!'

Zina cried and wordlessly squeezed his hands, as though by doing so she wanted to stop him.

'What are you crying about, my angel?' the sick man continued. 'About the fact that I'm dying, only about that? But all the rest died long ago, didn't it, it's long buried! You're cleverer than me, you're purer in heart, so you've known for a long time that I'm a bad man. Can you really still love me? And what it cost me to endure the idea that you knew I was a bad and shallow man! And how much self-esteem there was in me, perhaps even noble self-esteem... I don't know! Ah, my friend, my whole life has been a dream. I was forever dreaming, always dreaming, and I haven't lived, I was proud and despised the masses, but what was I so proud about in front of everyone? I don't know myself. Purity of heart, nobility of feelings? But that was all in dreams, you know, Zina, when we were reading Shakespeare, and when it came to deeds, then I really displayed my purity and nobility of feelings...'

'That's enough,' said Zina, 'that's enough!... this is all wrong, there's no point in it... you're killing yourself!'

'What are you stopping me for, Zina? I know you've forgiven me, and maybe you did so long ago; but you judged me and realised what I was; and that's what's tormenting me. I'm unworthy of your love, Zina! You were honest and magnanimous in deed as well: you went to your mother and said you'd marry me and no one else, and you would have kept your word, because your word was no different from your deed. But I, I! When it came to deeds... Do you know, Zinochka, I mean, I didn't even understand then what you were sacrificing in marrying me! I couldn't even understand the fact that, after marrying me, you might have died of hunger. How could I, it never even occurred to me! I mean, all I could think was that you were marrying me, a great poet (a future one, that is), and I didn't want to understand the reasons you put forward, when asking me to delay a little with the wedding, I tormented, tyrannised, reproached and scorned you, and finally reached the point of threatening you with that note. I wasn't even a cad at that moment. I was simply a scoundrel! Oh, how you must have despised me! No, it's a good thing that I'm dying! It's a good thing you didn't marry me! I would have understood nothing of your sacrifice, I'd have tormented you, tortured you over our poverty; the years would have gone by – and where to? – and maybe I would even have come to hate you as a hindrance in my life. But things are better now! Now, at least, my bitter tears have cleansed the heart within me. Ah, Zinochka! Love me, if only a little, the way you loved me before! If only in this final hour… I know I'm unworthy of your love, but… but… o my angel!'

Throughout the whole of this speech, Zina, sobbing herself, several times tried to stop him. But he wouldn't listen to her; he was tormented by the desire to speak his mind, and he continued to speak, albeit with difficulty, gasping for breath, in a hoarse, choking voice.

'If you hadn't met me, if you hadn't fallen in love with me, then you'd have remained alive!' said Zina. 'Ah, why, why did we come together?'

'No, my friend, no, don't reproach yourself because I'm dying,' the sick man continued. 'I alone am to blame for everything! There was so much self-esteem in me, so much romanticism! Have you been told my silly story in detail, Zina? You see, two years ago there was this prisoner here, a condemned man, a villain and murderer; but when it came to his punishment, he proved the most faint-hearted fellow. Knowing that a sick man wouldn't be taken to his punishment, he got hold of some wine, infused some tobacco in it and drank it. He began vomiting so, bringing up blood, and it continued for such a long time that it damaged his lungs. He was transferred to the hospital, and a few months later he died of acute consumption. Well, my angel, and so I remembered that prisoner on the very day… well, you know, after the note… and made up my mind to destroy myself the same way. But what do you think, why did I choose consumption? Why didn't I hang myself, drown myself? Was I afraid of a quick death? Maybe that's so – but it constantly seems to me somehow, Zinochka, that even in this I couldn't manage without some sweet romantic nonsense! After all, at the time I had the idea of how beautiful it would be: I'd be lying on a bed, dying of consumption, and you'd be grieving all the time, suffering, because you'd driven me to consumption; you'd come to me yourself with an admission of guilt, you'd drop to your knees before me… I forgive you, while dying in your arms… It's silly, Zinochka, silly, isn't it?'

'Don't recall it!' said Zina, 'don't say it! You're not like that… better, let's remember the other things, the good, happy things we had!'

'I feel bitter, my friend, that's why I'm saying it. I haven't seen you for a year and a half! I think I'd like to bare my soul before you now. I mean, all that time since then I've been by myself, and I don't think there's been a minute when I haven't been thinking of you, my beloved angel! And do you know what, Zinochka? How I wanted to do something, to atone somehow in such a way as to make you alter your opinion of me! Until recently I didn't believe I was going to die; after all, I wasn't laid low at once, I went around for a long time with a bad chest. And how many ridiculous intentions did I have! I dreamt, for example, of suddenly becoming some supreme poet, of publishing in *Notes of the Fatherland*[59] such a narrative poem as there had never before been on earth. I thought to pour out all my feelings in it, all my soul, so that, wherever you were, I would always be with you, would constantly remind you of myself with my verse, and my best dream of all was the one that you would finally become pensive and say: "No, he's not such a bad man as I thought!" It's silly, Zinochka, silly, isn't it?'

'No, no, Vasya, no!' said Zina.

She sank onto his breast and kissed his hands.

'And how jealous I've been of you all this time! I think I'd have died if I'd heard about you getting married! I've sent and had you watched, spied on you… she was always going' (and he nodded at his mother). 'You didn't love Mozglyakov, did you, Zinochka? O my angel? Will you remember me when I'm dead? I know you will; but the years will go by, your heart will cool, the cold and winter will set in in your soul, and you'll forget me, Zinochka!…'

'No, no, never! I shan't even marry!… You're my first… my abiding…'

'Everything dies, Zinochka, everything, even memories!… And our noble feelings die too. In their place, prudence sets in. Why even bemoan it? Make good use of life, Zina, live long, live happily. Fall in love with another man too, if someone takes your fancy – you can't go loving a dead man! Only do remember me, if only occasionally, don't remember the bad things, forgive the bad things; but there were good things in our love, you know, Zinochka! O golden, irretrievable days... Listen, my angel, I've always loved the evening, the hour of sunset. Remember me sometime at that hour! Oh no, no! Why die? Oh, how I'd love to come to life again now! Remember, my friend, remember, remember that time! It was spring then, the sun shone so brightly, the flowers were in bloom, it was like a celebration all around us... But now! Look, look!'

And the poor man pointed with a dried-up hand at the dull, frozen window. Then he grasped Zina's hands, pressed them to his eyes and began sobbing oh so bitterly. The sobbing almost ripped his tormented breast apart.

And all day long he suffered, lamented and cried. Zina comforted him as best she could, but her soul suffered mortally. She said she wouldn't forget him and that she would never love anyone as she had loved him. He believed her, smiled, kissed her hands, but recollections of the past only seared, only tortured his soul. A whole day passed like this.

Meanwhile, the frightened Maria Alexandrovna sent to Zina a dozen times, beseeching her to return home and not to completely ruin everyone's opinion of her. Finally, when it had already got dark, having almost lost her head in terror, she made up her mind to go to Zina herself. Summoning her daughter into the other room, she implored her almost on her knees to 'deflect this final and most crucial dagger away from her heart'. Zina came out to her unwell: her head was burning. She listened to her Mamma, but didn't understand her. Maria Alexandrovna finally went away in despair, because Zina had made up her mind to stay the night in the dying man's house. She didn't leave his bedside all night long. But the sick man was getting worse and worse.

Another day began, but no longer was there even any hope that the suffering man would live through it. His aged mother was like a madwoman, going around as though she understood nothing and giving her son medicines which he didn't want to take. His death throes lasted a long time. He could no longer speak, and only incoherent, hoarse sounds tore themselves from his breast. He kept on looking at

Zina until the very last minute, kept on seeking her out with his eyes, and when the light in his eyes had already begun to grow dim, he still kept on seeking with a wandering, uncertain hand for hers, to squeeze it in his own. Meanwhile, the short winter's day was passing. And when at last the final farewell ray of sunlight gilded the single little frozen window of the small room, the soul of the suffering man flew out from his exhausted body and away in the wake of that ray. His aged mother, finally seeing before her the corpse of her beloved Vasya, clasped her hands, cried out and threw herself upon the dead man's breast.

'It's you that destroyed him, you snake in the grass!' she shouted in despair at Zina. 'You that damned well came between us, you villainess, you that killed him!'

But Zina no longer heard a thing. She stood over the dead man as if out of her mind. Finally she bent and made the sign of the cross over him, kissed him and walked mechanically out of the room. Her eyes were burning, her head was spinning. Agonising emotions and two practically sleepless nights had all but deprived her of her reason. She vaguely felt that the whole of her past had somehow been torn away from her heart and a new life had begun, gloomy and threatening. But she had not gone ten paces before Mozglyakov seemed to rise up out of the ground in front of her. He appeared to have been deliberately lying in wait at this spot.

'Zinaida Afanasyevna,' he began in a fearful sort of whisper, hurriedly looking around on all sides, because it was still quite light, 'Zinaida Afanasyevna, of course, I'm an ass! That is, if you like, I'm actually no longer an ass now, because, you see, I've acted nobly after all. But nevertheless, I'm repentant about having been an ass… I seem to be getting confused, Zinaida Afanasyevna, but… forgive me, it's for various reasons…'

Zina looked at him almost unconsciously and continued in silence on her way. Since there wasn't room for two people next to one another on the raised wooden sidewalk, and Zina didn't move aside, Pavel Alexandrovich jumped off the sidewalk and ran alongside her down below, glancing continually into her face.

'Zinaida Afanasyevna,' he continued, 'I've considered things, and if you yourself want it, then I'm agreeable to renewing my proposal.

145

I'm even prepared to forget everything, Zinaida Afanasyevna, all the disgrace, and I'm prepared to forgive, but only on one condition: while we're here, everything remains in secret. You'll leave here as soon as possible; I'll quietly come after you; we'll marry somewhere in the back of beyond so that no one will see, and then to St Petersburg straight away, maybe even by post-chaise, so you should have only one little suitcase with you... eh? Do you agree, Zinaida Afanasyevna? Tell me, quickly! I can't wait; we might be seen together.'

Zina made no reply and just looked at Mozglyakov, but looked at him in such a way that he understood everything at once, took off his hat, bowed, and disappeared at the first turning into a side street.

'What's going on?' he thought. 'In the evening just two days ago wasn't she so moved, and blaming herself for everything? She's evidently never the same from one day to the next!'

But meanwhile, one occurrence followed another in Mordasov. And there was one tragic circumstance. The Prince, who had been taken by Mozglyakov to the hotel, that same night fell ill, dangerously ill too. The Mordasovans learnt of this in the morning. Kallist Stanislavich hardly left the sick man's bedside. Towards evening a consultation of all Mordasov's doctors was set up. Invitations were sent to them in Latin. But despite the Latin, the Prince lost consciousness completely, he was delirious, asked Kallist Stanislavich to sing him some romance or other and talked about wigs of some sort; he seemed at times to take fright at something and cried out. The doctors decided that Mordasov's hospitality had caused an inflammation in the Prince's stomach, which had somehow (probably en route) spread to his head. They didn't rule out a certain mental shock either. Their conclusion was that the Prince had already long been predisposed to die, and for that reason was bound to do so.

In the latter they were not mistaken, because towards evening on the third day the poor old man died in the hotel. This stunned the Mordasovans. Nobody had been expecting such a serious turn of events. People rushed in crowds to the hotel where the dead body lay, not as yet prepared for burial, they passed judgement, laid down the law, nodded their heads, and finished by sharply condemning 'the unfortunate Prince's murderers', implying by this, of course, Maria

Alexandrovna and her daughter. Everyone felt that this incident might, through its scandalous nature alone, receive unpleasant publicity, would quite likely even find its way to distant countries, and – everything under the sun was rehearsed and retold.

All this time Mozglyakov was bustling about, rushing in all directions, and finally his head started to spin. And that was the state of mind in which he met with Zina. His position really was a difficult one. He himself had brought the Prince to town, he himself had moved him to the hotel, and now he didn't even know what to do with the deceased, how to bury him and where, whom to let know. Should the body be taken to Dukhanovo? Moreover, he was considered a nephew. He was nervous that he might be blamed for the venerable old man's death. 'The matter may even be spoken of in St Petersburg, in high society!' he thought with a shudder. It was impossible to get any advice from the Mordasovans; everyone suddenly took fright at something, recoiled from the dead body, and left Mozglyakov in a sort of gloomy isolation.

But suddenly the whole scene quickly altered. The next day, early in the morning, a visitor drove into town. The whole of Mordasov instantly began talking about this visitor, but began talking mysteriously somehow, in a whisper, peeping out at him from every chink and window when he went down Bolshaya Street to see the Governor. Even Pyotr Mikhailovich himself seemed to lose his nerve a little and didn't know how to behave with his newly arrived guest. The guest was the quite well-known Prince Schepetilov, a relative of the deceased, a still almost young man of about thirty-five, wearing the epaulettes and aiguillettes of a colonel. Those aiguillettes struck an extraordinary sort of fear into the hearts of all the officials. The Chief of Police, for example, was quite lost; only mentally, it stands to reason; physically he showed his face, although his face was quite a long one. It was learnt straight away that Prince Schepetilov was travelling from St Petersburg and had dropped in at Dukhanovo on his way. Not finding anyone at Dukhanovo, he had flown after his uncle to Mordasov, where he had been thunderstruck by the old man's death and by all the highly detailed rumours about the circumstances of his death. Pyotr Mikhailovich even became a little confused, giving the necessary explanations; and everyone in Mordasov looked guilty somehow.

Moreover, the newly arrived guest had such a stern, such a displeased face, although, you would have thought, one can't be displeased about an inheritance. He at once got down to business himself, personally. And Mozglyakov immediately and shamefully removed himself in the face of a genuine, not a self-styled nephew, and vanished no one knew where. It was decided to transfer the body of the deceased immediately to a monastery, where the burial service was arranged too. All of the new arrival's instructions were issued briefly, dryly, sternly, but with tact and propriety.

On the following day the whole town prepared to go to the monastery to attend the funeral service. An absurd rumour spread amongst the ladies that Maria Alexandrovna would appear in person at the church and, on her knees before the coffin, would loudly solicit forgiveness for herself, and that it all had to be so according to law. It stands to reason, this all proved to be nonsense, and Maria Alexandrovna didn't appear at the church. We forgot to say that immediately upon Zina's return home, that same evening her Mamma made up her mind to move to the country, considering it more impossible to remain in town. There from her corner she listened anxiously to the rumours in town, sent people on reconnaissance missions to find out about the new arrival, and was all the time in a fever. The road from the monastery to Dukhanovo passed less than a verst from the windows of her country house, and so Maria Alexandrovna was comfortably able to make out the long procession stretching from the monastery towards Dukhanovo after the funeral service. The coffin was carried on a high hearse; behind it stretched a long line of conveyances, accompanying the deceased as far as the turning to town. And for a long time that gloomy hearse, drawn slowly with fitting grandeur, continued to show black against the snow-white fields. But Maria Alexandrovna couldn't look for long and moved away from the window.

A week later she moved to Moscow with her daughter and Afanasy Matveyich, and a month later it was learnt in Mordasov that Maria Alexandrovna's village outside of town and her town house were up for sale. And so Mordasov was losing such a *comme il faut* lady for ever! Even at this point people couldn't do without back-biting. They began averring, for example, that the village was for sale with Afanasy

Matveyjch included... A year passed, then another, and Maria Alexandrovna was almost completely forgotten. Alas! That's the way it always is in the world! It was said, incidentally, that she had bought herself another village and moved to the main town of another province, where, it stands to reason, she had already taken everyone in hand, that Zina was still not married, that Afanasy Matveyich... But anyway, there's no reason to repeat the rumours, it's all very uncertain.

* * *

Three years have passed since I finished writing the last line of the first section of the Mordasov chronicle, and who would have thought that I would be obliged to unfold my manuscript once more and add another piece of news to my story. But to business!

I'll begin with Pavel Alexandrovich Mozglyakov. After removing himself from Mordasov, he went straight off to St Petersburg, where he duly received the official position he had long been promised. He soon forgot all the events in Mordasov, and launched himself into the whirl of the social life of Vasilyevsky Island and the Galley Harbour,[60] he led a life of pleasure, ran after women, kept up with the times, fell in love, proposed, swallowed a refusal once again, and, failing to digest it, through the frivolity of his nature and for want of anything better to do, solicited a place for himself in an expedition which was being dispatched to one of the most remote regions of our boundless fatherland on a government inspection or for some other purpose, I don't know for sure.

The expedition travelled safely through all the forests and wildernesses and finally, after long wandering, in the main town of the 'most remote region' presented itself to the Governor-general. He was a tall, lean and stern general, an old warrior, battle-scarred, with two stars and a white cross at his neck. He received the expedition in formal and orderly fashion, and invited all the officials of which it was composed to a ball being given that same evening at his house on the occasion of the name-day of the Governor-general's wife. Pavel Alexandrovich was very pleased about this. Having dressed himself up in his St Petersburg costume, in which he intended to make an impact, he entered the big reception hall in a free-and-easy manner, although he was immediately a little disconcerted by the sight of the multitude of dense woven epaulettes and Civil Service dress uniforms with stars. He needed to pay his respects to the Governor-general's wife, who, he had already heard it said, was young and very good-looking. He even approached with a swagger, but suddenly he was rooted to the spot in amazement.

Before him stood Zina in a magnificent ball gown and diamonds, proud and haughty. She completely failed to recognise Pavel Alexandrovich. Her gaze slid carelessly across his face and immediately turned to someone else. The astonished Mozglyakov moved aside, and in the crowd bumped into a timid young official who, on finding himself at the Governor-general's ball, even seemed to be frightened of himself. Pavel Alexandrovich set about questioning him at once and found out some extremely interesting things. He found out that it was already two years since the Governor-general had got married, having gone to Moscow from the 'remote region', and that he had taken an extremely rich girl from a distinguished house. That the General's wife was 'terribly good *to look at*, sir, even, you might say, the leading beauty, sir, but conducts herself extremely proudly, and dances only with generals, sir'; that at the present ball there were in all nine generals, local and visiting ones, and including Actual State Councillors; that, finally, 'the General's wife has a Mamma, sir, who lives with her, and this Mamma came from the very highest society, sir, and is very clever, sir', but that even the Mamma herself submitted unquestioningly to the will of her daughter, while the Governor-general himself doted on the spouse who was the apple of his eye. Mozglyakov made some mention of Afanasy Matveyich, but in the 'remote region' they had no idea about him.

Slightly encouraged, Mozglyakov walked from room to room and soon saw Maria Alexandrovna too, magnificently attired, waving an expensive fan about, and talking animatedly with one of the fourth-class personages.[61] Around her clustered several ladies eager for patronage, and Maria Alexandrovna was apparently extraordinarily courteous with everyone. Mozglyakov took the risk of presenting himself. Maria Alexandrovna seemed to wince a little, but recovered straight away, almost instantly. She was courteously good enough to recognise

Pavel Alexandrovich; she asked about his acquaintanceships in St Petersburg, asked why he wasn't abroad. Of Mordasov she said not a word, as though it didn't even exist. Finally, after pronouncing the name of some important prince in St Petersburg and enquiring after his health, although Mozglyakov had no idea at all about this prince, she imperceptibly turned to a dignitary with fragrant grey hair[62] who had come up to her, and a minute later had forgotten all about Pavel Alexandrovich standing in front of her. With a sarcastic smile and his hat in his hands, Mozglyakov returned to the large reception hall. Considering himself for some unknown reason wounded, even insulted, he resolved not to dance. A morosely absentminded air, a caustic Mephistophelean smile never left his face the entire evening. He leant picturesquely against a column (the hall, as luck would have it, had columns), and for the duration of the entire ball, several hours running, he stood in the one spot, following Zina with his gaze. But alas! All his tricks, all his extraordinary poses, his disenchanted air, and so on, and so forth – all was wasted. Zina didn't notice him at all. Finally, infuriated, with legs that ached from standing for so long, hungry – because, as a man in love and suffering, he couldn't, of course, stay for supper – he returned to his quarters, completely worn out and feeling as though someone had given him a beating. He didn't go to bed for some time, remembering things that had been long forgotten. The very next morning, some sort of official trip presented itself, and Mozglyakov was delighted to get himself assigned to it. His soul even felt refreshed when he had left town. On the endless, deserted expanse lay a dazzling shroud of snow. At its edge, at the very slope of the sky, forests showed black.

The zealous steeds raced ahead, turning up the snowy dust with their hooves. The sleigh-bell rang. Pavel Alexandrovich fell into thought, then fell to dreaming, and then very quietly fell asleep. He woke up when already at the third posting-station, fresh and healthy, with completely different thoughts.

NOTES

1. The reference is to the calamitous earthquake of 1755.

2. Here 'ladylike behaviour' (French)

3. Giuseppe Pinetti (1750–1800), Italian conjuror and magician at the French court, he died in Russia.

4. 'Gentleman' (French)

5. A verst is a Russian measure of length approximately equal to one kilometre.

6. A reactionary Russian newspaper published in St Petersburg between 1825 and 1864.

7. 'Good day, my friend, good day!' (French)

8. 'That poor Prince!' (French)

9. A misquotation of a line from Chapter 1 of Alexander Pushkin's *Eugene Onegin* (1823–31).

10. Afanasy Afanasyevich Fet (1820–92) was a major lyric poet to whom Mozglyakov seems wrongly to ascribe Pushkin's line (see note 9).

11. Another inaccurate attribution, this time to the German poet and essayist Heinrich Heine (1797–1856).

12. 'A very nice story' (German)

13. 'My dear Paul' (French)

14. 'That's delightful!' (French)

15. 'That's charming!' (French)

16. 'But what a beauty!' (French)

17. German philosopher Immanuel Kant (1724–1804).

18. Here 'correctness' (French)

19. Three of Russia's classic authors of comedy: Denis Ivanovich Fonvizin (1745–92), Alexander Sergeyevich Griboyedov (1795–1829) and Nikolai Vasilyevich Gogol (1809–52).

20. The story is set at the time of the Crimean War (1853–6).

21. The Congress of Vienna took place between September 1814 and June 1815 following the initial abdication of Napoleon Bonaparte; the poet Lord Byron (1788–1824) was not a participant.

22. 'It's an idea no worse than any other!' (French)

23. 'That's nice' (French)

24. The name may be derived from the French verb *gribouiller*, to daub, or the noun *un gribouille*, a simpleton.

25. An anonymously written vaudeville, popular in St Petersburg in 1845, a literal translation of whose title is *The Husband's through the Door and the Wife's off to Tver*.

26. 'Goodbye, Madam, farewell, my charming young lady' (French)

27. 'My child' (French)

28. A popular literary journal published in St Petersburg between 1834 and 1865, in which very little poetry of any note appeared in the 1850s.

29. Jean Pierre Claris de Florian (1755–94), French author of novels, fables and pastorals.

30. 'My angel' (French)

31. She means Majorca, renowned in the nineteenth century for the healing qualities of its climate.

32. 'You understand' (French)

33. A misuse of the French phrase meaning 'my pleasure'.

34. 'But my dear' (French)

35. 'How dreadful!' (French)

36. 'In a grand style' (French)

37. 'Beautiful woman' (French)

38. 'But what a charming individual!' (French)

39. 'O my charming child! […] You enrapture me!' (French)

40. Ivan Stepanovich Mazepa (1644–1709) was hetman of the Cossacks from 1687, and Maria is the much younger heroine of Pushkin's narrative poem *Poltava* (1829) who falls in love with him.

41. Antoine de Caumont, Duke of Lauzun (1633–1723), was a soldier and courtier under Louis XIV of France and was renowned for his involvement in court intrigues.

42. 'The Swallow' (French). This, like the other romance referred to in this passage, is on such a common theme for such works that identification is impossible.

43. 'O my beautiful lady of the castle!' (French)

44. Literally 'early in the morning' (German). While in Siberia Dostoevsky noted down the expression (which in Russian rhymes) 'early in the morning – wipe your nose'

45. She probably has in mind Johann Strauss the younger (1825–99), who performed in Russia with great success in 1856.

46. Two French novels, *The Count of Monte Cristo* (1844) by Alexandre Dumas *père* (1802–70), and *The Devil's Memoirs* (1837–38) by Frédéric Soulié (1800–47).

47. 'Word of honour, my friend!' (French)

48. 'Full-face' (French)

49. After his defeat at Waterloo, Napoleon surrendered to the British and was exiled to St Helena, where he died in 1821.

50. 'She's a charming individual' (French)

51. 'This beautiful individual' (French)

52. The memoirs of the Italian adventurer Giovanni Jacopo Casanova (1725–98) were published in Leipzig in twelve volumes between 1828 and 1838.

53. 'But my charming girl' (French)

54. 'For the health' (French)

55. 'What an abominable woman!' (French)

56. 'A bourgeois family, but an honest one' (French)

57. She evidently has in mind the period of Louis XIV's infancy when Anne of Austria was queen-regent in France, described most memorably by Dumas in *Twenty Years After* (1845); Fairelacour is an invented name from the French phrase meaning 'to pay court'; on Lauzun see note 41.

58. 'What society!' (French)

59. A respected, long-running literary journal published in St Petersburg between 1818 and 1884.

60. Socially, these were two very modest areas of the capital.

61. The fourth class in the Civil Service, Actual State Councillor, was equivalent to the army rank of Major-General.

62. The phrase is taken from the ball scene in the final chapter of Pushkin's *Eugene Onegin*, of which Dostoevsky's ball scene here is a parody.

BIOGRAPHICAL NOTE

Fyodor Mikhailovich Dostoevsky (1812–81) was born in Moscow. After the death of his mother in 1837, he was sent to the St Petersburg Engineering Academy, where he studied for five years and eventually graduated as an engineer. In 1844, however, Dostoevsky gave up engineering to write. His translation of Balzac's *Eugénie Grandet* came out in 1844, and his first novel, *Poor People*, was published in 1846. During this time Dostoevsky also became interested in Utopian Socialism – a political affiliation that would lead to his deportation, in 1850, to Siberia. He was imprisoned for four years in a penal settlement, and served for four more thereafter as a soldier in Semipalatinsk. The experience changed his life and writing: whilst in prison he became a member of the Russian Orthodox Church, a monarchist, and upon his return to Moscow, he wrote about his experience as a prisoner in *Notes from the House of the Dead* (1862).

In 1862, Dostoevsky travelled around Europe for the first time, an experience that also marked his writing. He was a great admirer of the English novel, in particular the works of Charles Dickens, but he disliked Europe. London, above all, was Dostoevsky's 'Baal', the centre of world capitalism, and he used the Crystal Palace as a symbol of the corrupting influence of modernity in *Notes from the Underground* (1864). Upon his return to Russia, Dostoevsky wrote some of his best novels, including *Crime and Punishment* (1866), *The Idiot* (1868) and *The Karamazov Brothers* (1880), which he completed just before his death.

Having been largely ignored by English language readers in the nineteenth century, Dostoevsky is now considered to be the most popular and influential Russian author read in the twentieth and twenty-first centuries. The penetrating psychological nature of Dostoevsky's novels, his obsessive grappling with conscience, guilt and God, as well as the brilliance of his characterisation and plots, continue to inspire new generations of readers, writers and thinkers. Dostoevsky's novels are undisputed masterpieces.

Hugh Aplin studied Russian at the University of East Anglia and Voronezh State University, and worked at the Universities of Leeds and St Andrews before taking up his current post as Head of Russian at Westminster School, London. His previous translations include Nikolai Gogol's *The Squabble*, Yevgeny Zamyatin's *We*, M. Ageyev's *A Romance with Cocaine*, and Yuri Olesha's *The Three Fat Men*, all published by Hesperus Press.